Chapter One

A Valet's Life Ain't Easy

It was quiet now. The smell of gunpowder was still distinct in the air, it stood in contrast to the tranquility of the night, a reminder of the violence of a few moments past. He was laying in an ocean of his own blood, in the dim light it looked black, like oil or tar. His eyes were wide open and he was taking shallow, rapid breaths. The end was not far.

He looked at me, but couldn't speak. With a last effort he reached for a nine millimeter lying on the ground next to him. Instinctively, I kicked it away. I felt some pity well up inside me, it was a life, a *human* life that was ending. He had made some poor choices to end up here, like this. I wonder though, had I lived his life would I have made the same? I never even considered calling for help. He was beyond help, just about the time I heard the sirens off in the distance, his chest stopped moving. Those glassy, cold eyes were staring straight at me, but now they saw nothing. I didn't need to check his pulse to know that he was dead.

This was the night that it all began in earnest, the night that the proverbial band-aid was ripped off, but I did a lot of pulling one hair length at a time before then...

My name is Andy Davis and I am a valet or at least I was. Six months before that night, things started to change. I don't know what set it all in motion exactly, but I suppose there comes a time in one of the many revolutions around our quaint little star floating in a sea of nothing, when a man needs a moment of self reflection. I chose my 25th, though in many ways it chose me.

Change is happening around us all the time and every generation seems to be a little bit different than the last. In order to make sense of these changes, we come up with cute little slogans like : "Thirty is the new twenty." or "Forty is the new thirty." I didn't feel like a new anything at twenty-five. I felt worn and used and just about done revolving in this sea of nothing altogether. I often wondered why everyone else was so happy. Were they? Or did they just appear that way? I was almost never happy. Like everyone of my generation I expected great things, I believed innately that my life would be better than those of my parents. I expected the world, though mostly I was only willing to "wish" for it. I hadn't had any real success in life. I knew there was some undefinably-better life out there, but I didn't know where to begin to make it happen. This frustrated me to no end. I had been fighting this feeling for years. The only thing that was keeping me from killing myself was my own irrational fear of death. How ridiculous, to fear losing something that you care so little about? As it turns out, people who are contemplating suicide often have low self-esteems; now I was a coward to boot. How much lower could I go?

The dark clouds above were threatening rain. You become very observant of the weather when you work outdoors.   I was a blue collar stiff, a working man, not a *hard* working man mind you, but a working man all the same. I was the lowest of the low, a valet. I parked cars for rich people. Before I started this job I was under the impression that people were generally good and it was just a few bad apples that ruin the reputation of the human race. I couldn't have been more wrong, there may be nice people in the world but none of them valet park. It's like having a job with a thousand different bosses, all of whom treat you like something far less than human. They pay you a dollar to run like a dog at the track. Sometimes I picture a mechanical bunny just out of reach as I sprint until my lungs catch fire and my legs want to explode, all for a dollar...sometimes. It's not at all uncommon for me to get nothing, I've even gotten pretty good at predicting a stiff, the house-wife in the Porsche with the new boob job...no tip, she's probably never had a job, in fact anyone that drives a Porsche at all, it's like you have to show some kind of card that proves how big of a douche bag you are before they will even sell you one. Your best bet is a young professional driving a Honda. It's like he's got a little money now, but remembers what it was like bussing tables before he went to law school. Foreigners, especially Asians are a bad bet, though most of the time they don't know any better, so it's hard to fault them. The sign says five bucks so they pay five bucks. It makes sense. Come to think of it, tipping is pretty much bullshit. Why should they have to pay my wage? It's a weird job; I constantly have a song in my head. Every time I jump into a car there's a new one on the radio by the pop-princess of the week, either that or some hate-radio cleverly disguised as political banter. Why were people so damn political anyway? I read bumper stickers all day long and everyone's got something to say about what they think is awesome. I wonder if anyone's mind has *ever* been changed by a bumper sticker? Like you read it and all of the sudden a light goes on in your head, "Hmm...never thought about it before, I guess I *should* recycle." Besides, I never asked for your opinion, you're just telling me. I feel like bumper stickers are shouting at me: "Namaste...Mother@#$%!...Jesus Saves...Dumb@#$... Coexist...Bitch! Half the time I don't even know what they are saying, "Pro Life" they exclaim! What does that mean? So I suppose you're a vegetarian? Oh no? Hmm? You must be against capital punishment? I hear you, an eye for an eye leaves everyone blind. Oh, you're not?...ok well then you're obviously one of those damn peacenik-pacifists who wouldn't raise a gun against any enemy...what's that you say? I'm wrong again? So we're starting to get pretty specific here, what kind of life are you pro? Their counterparts fight ambiguity with ambiguity, "Pro-choice"? Who doesn't want choices? Why stop there, how about pro-happiness, pro-sunshine, pro-good, it makes about as much damn sense. I feel like Diane Fossey, lost in some remote jungle, but instead of studying gorillas, I serve them. I am surrounded by idiots and yet all of them have more than I. In the end who's really the idiot? (Sigh) Where was I? Oh yes, I parked cars at Farlaino's Italian restaurant, a very posh dining establishment right smack dab in the middle of Salt Lake City, Utah. If you've never been to this fine metropolis, I recommend checking it out, not because it's a great place necessarily, though the snow capped peaks of the Wasatch Mountain range do offer moments of aesthetic delight. Don't come here for the culture or the night life. The people are ok I suppose, though I've met very few whom I would suggest getting to know. There are my parents and my best friend John, a handful of others, but not a large number. No, I would recommend this city because it's a case study, a microcosm of the American dream. It's all shiny and new, full of smiling faces and insincere laughs. A gilded city. I think that everyone here is just as depressed as I, they just hide behind their pharmaceutical masks. I didn't take drugs, I guess I felt that it was better to be depressed in reality than happily removed from it. For that matter, I wasn't religious either. Which was pretty uncommon around here. Yes, my home town is a case study indeed, but not the focus of my story.

The wind began to pick up a bit now, the rain would not be far behind, it never was.

"This day couldn't get any worse," I thought to myself. My mind drifted briefly to my friend Carter, an adventurous sort, whom I roomed with in college. Carter had left the whole rat-race behind and moved to Puerto Rico. He went there for vacation and just... stayed. Who the hell does that? Last I heard he was tending bar at some bungalow on an island off the coast called Isla Mona. I could only imagine what he was doing right now, probably smoking a big joint and swimming with the dolphins. I briefly hated him. Not just because regardless of what he was doing he was no doubt warm, but because he had the courage to just *do* things.

He never talked, he just acted. Everyone else just sits around and makes up excuses as to why they don't change things when they are unhappy. I know I could fill a warehouse with mine.

A crack of thunder and right on cue the rain began to fall. Yup, this day couldn't get any worse. Farlaino's had an awning that was great for these kinds of situations. I flipped up the hood of my jacket and found a nice wall to hold up near the entrance to the restaurant. It was slow tonight, even for a weekday. In the service industry it's always better to work when you're at work. When you're working for tips you don't get paid unless you do, plus running back and forth to the lot kept me warm. A silver SUV pulled up to the podium. On impulse I jumped into action and ran to the car, ticket in hand, realizing only at the last moment that this wasn't a customer. It was my boss, Denis...and I thought this day couldn't get any worse.

Denis was the manager of my valet company. He was a well-dressed, over-weight, white guy, with the look and demeanor of a frat-boy now thirty. Denis was one of those chubby guys who just wont concede the fact, believing that he was in as good a shape now as when he was in high school. He could bench press 250 pounds. I know this, because he told me all the time and he was supposedly quite the football player back in the day. I suspect that both of these stories were exaggerations, if not outright lies.

  Denis's job consisted mostly of driving around in his car and making sure that all of us valets were actually working and that none of us were stealing, a not uncommon practice among the people of the industry. He rolled down his window and propped his hand up in a position so that I could see his new watch. This one was plain and kind of boring, but said "Gucci" in big letters across the face. I hated Denis too, but never briefly. Denis loved watches, he spent most of his money on watches and the rest he spent on weed and blow or so was the common conception. I had worked many a shift with co-workers who would jump into that car with Denis, take a ride with him only to come back with a slightly more congenial attitude toward being at work and that half grin of a stoner that is always on the verge of laughter. I never did drugs with him, I think he resented me for it.

"How's it going tonight?"
Denis spoke, as he adjusted the strap to his watch.

"Kind of slow, I've got about a half-dozen cars."

Denis wasn't really interested, what he really wanted was for me to compliment him on his watch. I hated his watch! That watch cost more than I made in a month. I was taking a stand, I would not say anything about his stupid watch.

"It'll pick up." he mused.

"Yeah, probably" I said with a shrug. Denis replied without taking his eyes from his newest toy.

"Hey listen, if you could stand next to the podium that would be great, it just looks more professional ya know."

"Yeah, I know, normally I would, but it's raining pretty hard and our umbrella's still broken."

Denis looked up to notice the rain for the very first time.

"Yeah, I'll have to work on getting you a new one, but for now if you could just grin and bear it, I'd appreciate it."

The rain continued to fall, even faster and it was starting to soak through my hood. We had an umbrella before, but a homeless guy had gotten mad at me because I didn't have any change to give him, he pushed over my lock box that we store the keys in and my umbrella had broken. That was two months ago now. I'd heard Denis's promise to get me a new one at least a dozen times since then. God, I hated that job. I'd been working there for three years and never had a raise, I'd never asked and they'd never offered. I tried to avoid confrontation as much as possible, but I'd been a good employee, in spite of the fact that I couldn't always hide my disdain for the customers and the general apathy that I approached life with. It was high time I got a raise, a little buttering up couldn't hurt.

"Nice watch." I said.
(I am such a pussy)

Denis smiled broadly and fiddled with his watch again.

"You like it? I couldn't decide, it's a simple design, but Gucci makes good watches."

What I wanted to tell him is that Gucci doesn't make watches and it was probably made by Timex and then they slapped a Gucci logo on the front so they could charge pretentious cocksuckers like him a cool grand, just so people would know that he has so much money he can afford to blow it on a stupid watch!

"It's really nice" I said.
(I am so pathetic)

"Thanks. Well I've got to get going, check on the other locations."

He was eager to leave now that he'd gotten the compliment he'd come for.

"Later" I said.

His silver SUV pulled away down the street and disappeared around the corner.

I took my position in front of the podium, soaking wet and freezing, I watched the gutters fill with water. A piece of paper floated aimlessly down the gutter on its way to the drain, for a moment it looked just like a sailboat heading for disaster. I'd always wanted to own a boat.

When I was younger, my father had once told me, "Be careful what you wish for, because you'll probably get it." At the time I thought it was just some of that, sometimes useful, dad advice that doesn't really mean much. At this point I had decided that it wasn't true at all. I can't remember wishing for anything like the life that I had constructed. Maybe I was doing it subconsciously? Maybe I really did want this life? A lot of guys my age were settling down and starting families. I had no interest in this for a couple of reasons. For one, I had no girl, which is a definite prerequisite. The other part of it was that I wasn't convinced that having kids was the best idea. I could barely take care of myself and hadn't figured out a thing about life, what would I possibly teach it? On a global scale, I often thought how there are starving children around the world. This being true, that meant that there were already more people in the world than food to feed them, so in some weird way every time a new baby is born another one dies somewhere, probably in Africa, bad shit is always happening to them. When I thought further, American kids take up far more than the average human in resources, so it was more likely that every time an American baby was born seven or eight babies starved to death! Heaven help us if that kid turned out to be obese, it could be tantamount to third world genocide! I'm not sure I could live with that kind of guilt. I don't know if the numbers added up exactly, but I felt like the logic was sound...but I digress, nope no family for me.

I was alone, my twenties were half-gone and life after college had only gotten progressively worse. I'm painting a pretty dismal picture here, but just trying to tell the story as accurately as possible. It wasn't all bad. This isn't one of those broken home kind of sob stories. I grew up in a nice family and had great parents, they cared about me and worried about me. The latter I felt that they did a little too much. Nobody needs the constant worry of their parents hanging over their heads.

I lived in a low rent apartment on the east side. It was small and dark, as it was in the basement of a house that had been turned into a small complex. I lived alone, had a lawn chair in the living room and a TV stand made out of boards and cinder blocks. This housed my 13' inch TV that was never on. I didn't watch TV. I couldn't understand the popularity of the reality shows that were taking over and I wasn't much for sports or anything. I spent most of my time reading and writing in my journal. It's funny that I had anything to write at all considering how boring I felt my world was.

The highlight of my night was listening to the people upstairs do it. The girl was a screamer and liked to be spanked. I'd met her before, her name was Rachel and she was friendly, always said "hi" to me when I passed her going to and from the apartment. I never caught the guy's name, but he didn't seem too interested in getting to know my name either. He was good looking and buff and all that and seemed to bring different girls home with some frequency. I wonder if Rachel knew. I some how doubt it. Such a sweet girl too, I could never understand why girls were always attracted to such jerks. I had never been much of a ladies' man. I thought of myself as handsome but not wildly attractive, though that seemed to matter less to women than it did to men. They liked the loud ones and the rich ones, which often went hand in hand. I was just the quiet one. I never understood why people were so willing to give their opinion, even when no one asked. Add that to the list of things I didn't understand, right below women in general.

    This night, Rachel and the jerk were being particularly loud. The sounds of the spanking and the moans and groans were oddly both arousing and annoying. It was hard for me to concentrate. I needed to get out of the house. I grabbed my beat up black leather jacket and headed for the door. It was dark out, well, as dark as it ever gets in the city, but dark enough that I could plainly see starlight cutting through the city haze. I loved to look up at the night sky. I don't know if it was more to appreciate its depth or relate to its emptiness. The sheer magnitude of space both intrigued and exhilarated me and left me feeling small and alone. It also served to distract me from the present and made my mind wander to new and interesting places, which I liked.

    I did this sometimes, just went for walks; it didn't seem like that common of a past time for most. I thought it would be a good thing for all, what with all our kids being a bit on the round side these days. When I went to school, there was one fat kid, everybody knew him because he was "the" fat kid. My fat kids name was Rhet. I knew this guy in junior high named Chuck who used to make fun of Rhet relentlessly, used to call him names like Rhet the jet, or blimpy. As one could imagine, Rhet was not very fast, so the jet was meant to be ironic and blimps were big and wide just like Rhet so that was meant to be sincere. It was lost to Chuck that both of them were modes of air transportation, one fast and one slow, which ended up being a bit of a contradiction and somewhat of an irony in itself. It seems as though a lot was lost to Chuck. He didn't know much, but what he would find out is what it's like to get beat up by a fat kid in front of the whole school. One day, it seems as though Rhet had had enough, Chuck walked up behind Rhet and knocked his books out of his hands. "Oops" he said. With a stupid grin, that can only be pulled off by the truly confident...and stupid. Without a word Rhet turned around and threw a hay-maker right into Chuck's grill knocking that grin off his face and him to the floor. Rhet fell right on top of him, the fight was over from there. Chuck would have had a better chance moving time backwards than Rhet from his chest. Rhet continued to rain punches down on Chuck, fourteen years of rage released in a single moment. It was like watching the liberation of a soul, the birth of a man and the unveiling of the frightened child that Chuck really was. Chuck was crying and his face was bloodied and bruised. To add insult to injury his girlfriend had shown up and was trying to save him by screaming obscenities and hitting Rhet on the back with her purse. The whole school had gathered around to watch this display. It was like a train wreck or the Superbowl you had to watch even if you didn't want to. After an eternity a teacher saw them and broke it up. Rhet had to take a few days off from school, but when he returned, something had changed. He was confident and funny like no one had ever noticed before. That was the last time that anyone ever picked on Rhet. There was a lesson in there somewhere I'm sure; maybe that overconfidence can be a problem...it certainly wasn't mine.

I had a loop that I would do that took me past Liberty Park, it was a nice big park with a pond in the middle and not completely over run with homeless people, not that I mind homeless people so much, but working outside in a city, I got hit up for change at least ten times a shift.

There were a lot of joggers out. There always were this time of year, give them a week and most of them would forget their new year's resolution for getting in shape, likely in favor of a reality TV show about people getting in shape. Then this park would be quiet again. My phone rang. I answered it:

"Hello?"

"How's my favorite cracker?"

The voice on the other side said, in that undefinably black voice. I thought that I could tell black people by the sound of their voice on the phone. I've never told anyone this and used to wonder a lot whether someone would consider it racist. I wasn't a racist, at least I didn't think I was. This guy on the phone was John Daniels. If I had a best friend it was John…and he was black.

"Hey John, how's it goin?" I said in my best attempt at the voice of a man not living a life of quiet desperation.

"Man, you sound like you just lost your best friend, where are you?"

(I am an open book).

"The park" I said.

"I'm right near there, meet me at the basketball courts, I'll pick you up."

"Yeah, ok"

"Cool, peace."

I wasn't much in the mood for company, but John had a way of making all of my problems seem very trivial and most of the time he was right.

Now I know this may surprise a few people, but there is not a lot of color in Salt Lake City, the sighting of a black man here is on par with a Bigfoot sighting in the Pacific Northwest or Nessy in Scotland. They were real though and you did see one once in a while and no matter how hard you tried you couldn't help notice them when they walked by. Most of the people here would side step them, not to be rude I don't think, mostly because they were scared and also because they were constantly struggling between acting like they didn't notice a black person had just crossed their path and trying not to be rude by staring at such a strange occurrence.

People stepped out of John's way all the time, not only because he was black, but because he was huge. John stood about 6'4" and weighed in about 230 pounds. We had met in college when he was the starting tight end for our football team. We lived in the dorms together our freshman year and we'd been friends ever since. He was gregarious and funny and everyone who met JD instantly liked him. He always had a great story to tell about some exotic trip he'd taken. JD had traveled a lot growing up. A fact that I was in complete envy of, to say the very least. The girls loved him and he loved them right back, he became quite the campus legend when we were roommates. More often than not I came home to a sock on the door indicating that the room was occupied. I spent most of that year on the couch, which I didn't mind really as I slept better on it than I did on those terrible twenty year old twin mattresses they used to put in our rooms.

    John's father was a bit of an accomplished poet and black activist in the sixties, Julian T. Daniels, he was super smart and talented and as is common was also depressed. One time he went into the bathroom and didn't come out for six hours, John was only ten, but he called the police, they came in broke down the door and caught John's father in the middle of one of those "cry for help" suicides, he stood up with a razor blade in hand, that was enough for those cops to unload two clips into him. No one heard his cry for help, Julian T. Daniels died that day. After the funeral John went to live with his Aunt and Uncle in New York. I always wondered if they'd have been as quick to fire if he was a white guy?

Chapter Two

The Plan

John picked me up from the park and we decided to grab a cup of coffee at Ruth's diner, an all night dive we used to frequent back in school. This was the kind of place, with those waitresses who were far too old to be working the 10-2 A.M. shift on a Friday night. Our waitress was a woman named Sally. She looked like she'd had a few too many years of late nights smoking cigarettes, the kind of person who makes you feel sorry for them just because they had so much potential at one time and then, through a series of bad choices, had let their youth slip away and now were left with three kids, a couple of Ex's, a job on the night shift and a $50.00 dollar a day meth habit. John interrupted my gaze that must have been longer than it felt.

"Yo Andy"

He snapped his fingers in front of my face.

"What are you looking at? You know experience counts for something, but I am sure you can do much better."

"What?" I fumbled.

"Nothin man, just teasing you, you were staring at that waitress a long time"

"Oh, yeah. Just thinking."

"What's on your mind man, you look like a troubled brother."

"I'm all right man, really."

John gave me a long glance before he began, one of those fatherly looks that says: "I know something's wrong and you don't want to talk about it. Cool, but we will talk about it later."

Some idle chit chat should suffice.

"If you were a superhero, what would you do?" I asked.

"There are no black superheroes." He said with a smirk.

"There aren't?"

JD shrugged his shoulders.

"Not that I can think of, What about you?" He asked.

"If I were a superhero, I wouldn't waste my time fighting crime one event at a time. Think about that on the scale of a city the size of New York, you'd hardly make any difference at all. No, what would work better is if you used your powers to steal money, and then use that money to make more money and influence the policy of government either by bribing officials, lobbying or even running for office."

"Yeah, that's sounds great, only one problem." He said.

"What's that?

"That's not a superhero, that's a villain."

"Really?"

"Yup."

"Oh."

JD sipped his coffee and the conversation stalled for a moment, before I filled the void again.

"How's your job?" I asked.

John was a bit of a drifter like me, he just found a way to drift through it all with a bit more enthusiasm than I did. He had graduated with me and gotten his degree in Math, he was a sharp guy with an affinity for numbers. All of the talents and optimism that John possessed aside, he was also a blue collar hack and hated his job as much as I hated mine, though he wouldn't talk about it unless he was asked. John worked for the city cutting tree branches away from power lines. It was a shit job, but he got to work outdoors, which he preached was important to him and he got benefits which I did not. It was good for him because there were a fair number of moments at a job like that where a medical plan comes in handy. He suffered from vertigo and neck pain, stemming from a mild electrocution he'd received last year.

"Man I will tell you what..." John began.

" I've got to find me a new line of work, the pay just isn't worth it anymore. A tree branch broke off above me today, nearly took my head clean off."

"Bummer" I added with a smile.

" One of these days that branch is going to fall off and hit a power line and bam just like that, one fried nigga."

"You think that smells anything like fried chicken?" I joked.

"Fuck you." He shot back.

JD was trying to keep a straight face, but couldn't help from laughing.

"What about you? Your life so great that you're wandering around the park at night, all alone and brooding. Where I grew up a white boy could get killed for doing that."

"I like it, helps me think."

"Oh really? What do you think about?"

"I don't know...Life, the universe, everything."

"Cute, Douglas Adams right?"
(John reads a lot).

"It's a good book."

I tried to change the subject, but John wasn't having it.

"Right. So how's your job Andy?"

An inadvertent sigh and frown was my body's response to this question as a precursor to my reply.

" I am having serious trouble keeping down my misanthropic tendencies."

"You hate people?" John asked with genuine curiosity.

" I can't help it, I know that there are good people in the world, or at least I want to believe that. If there are though, they never come to my restaurant. These old rich assholes come into my place and act like I'm doing them a favor by parking their car. I get paid to run, I'm no longer human. I'm like a fucking quarter horse and what do I get in compensation? A one bedroom shit-hole apartment, a pile of student loan debt that I can't possibly repay and the hope that I never have a serious injury, because if I do I'll be indentured for the rest of my life. So most days I wake up wondering why this life is even worth living."

I crossed a line.

It wasn't that I never thought about suicide. I thought about it all the time, but I never spoke of it out loud. JD in particular, took this type of talk very seriously. I looked down at the table and fiddled with a fork that I had picked up in the middle of my rant. John didn't say anything for a long time. He just looked at me for what felt like an eternity. I felt so small at that moment, I wanted him to speak, to say anything. Eventually he did.

"We need to get you out of here."

"What?"

"I've got a friend, he works for the air lines, can get us cheap tickets anywhere we want to go."

"Yeah, yeah. OK"

"Good, now that that's settled, where do you want to go?"

"Peru." I blurted out.

"Peru? Why Peru?"

"It's not here."

JD smiled a warm, broad smile and gave a chuckle.

"All right, South America it is then."

JD extended his big paw and I slapped it. All events begin with thought and are followed by action and even though I was still sitting in that diner on the east side of Salt Lake City, things had changed. I was on my way somewhere far away, I was on my way to Peru.

One decent part about working part time is that it does afford you a fair amount of time off, if you require it. You don't get paid a livable wage, but you can just bail on a moment's notice and I've discovered, even if you do happen to get fired because of your decision, there's always another low paying shitty service job that needs to be filled. John's friend Tye certainly hooked us up, we got on these buddy passes for the cost of fuel and that's it. We had our tickets for a steal and because the empty seats that needed to be filled were almost always in first class, that is exactly where we ended up.

Later on I would look up the ticket prices for the seats that we had and turns out they were going for close to five grand a piece. John and I had paid just over 200 bucks, round trip!

The sun was just cresting Mount Olympus on the Wasatch mountain range, it really was beautiful. It was about 7:30 a.m. and the dawn of a new day. I had never flown before and though I was acting like it was no big deal, my heart was racing the first time those jets fired up to send us racing down that runway. I know it shouldn't, but it still amazes me that they can get those giant tin cans up in the air. I was watching out the window as we cruised over the Great Salt Lake, I always forget how big it is, even though I've been living near it for most of my life. A giant, dead lake. No fish, only tiny little brine-shrimp, that weren't good for eating or anything. They mostly just made the lake smell like dead things. This is why The Great Salt Lake is not much of a tourist attraction, bad for swimming, no fishing and it smelled bad. All that being said if you ever get a chance to see it from the air, I'd take it. On this day I was mesmerized by the morning sun shining off the lake like a mirror presenting me with the mirage of two horizons. The beauty briefly took away my anxiety at being a couple of thousand feet in the air. John brought me back.

"How about this?! You're doing it man, leaving the country for the very first time. How does it feel?"

I just shrugged my shoulders, thinking that any speech at that moment may make my voice crack and expose the falseness of my calm demeanor. I was amazingly good at hiding my feelings, at pretending to be something that I was not, something that would serve me well throughout my days.

"That excited, huh?" John teased.

While John had traveled a lot as a kid and bounced around the country when he played football, he was delighted to be making his first trip to the southern hemisphere and so was I.

Before I could respond, the flight attendant had arrived with our first of many rounds of snacks and drinks. Flying first class is this ridiculous display of service, seemingly everyone has his very own flight attendant who is serving you every second of the time that you're in the air. I had a four hour flight to Atlanta and then another five hours to Lima. This was the most attention I'd had from a woman in years, or possibly ever. Our personal attendant's name was Katie and she was an adorable little blonde, couldn't have been a day over twenty-one and if she wasn't the friendliest woman I'd ever met, she was damn good at faking it. It didn't hurt one bit that JD had started to lay on his charm from the very first moment. If she didn't have to turn around and fly back to the states that same night, I thought that she may very well have accompanied us on all of our travels. She didn't, but she did bring us everything we needed and more; hot towels, deserts, wine, wine and more wine. By the time that we touched down in Atlanta, JD and I were a couple of silly drunks.

After a brief time of loading new passengers in Atlanta, we were back in the air. I must admit that my whole life I had believed that Atlanta was on the ocean, an idea that I had kept to myself so no one was aware of my geographic ignorance. Another one of those times, I thought that being quiet can sometimes lead people to the conclusion that you know more than you actually do. Regardless of where Atlanta was on earth, in relation to me it was getting further away by the second and JD and I were getting further away from sobriety. I'm not ordinarily a big drinker, but when you're riding first class all of the drinks are free, well free if you forget that you'd paid five grand for the ticket. These drinks tasted all the sweeter because we ,in fact, had not. As the night wore on, I busied myself with a computerized quiz game that was a part of the monitor embedded in the seat in front of me. I chose that over the in flight movie. This one was some feel good movie about ponies or something. JD assured me, that while pretty much everything was better about flying first class, the movies were just as bad as they were in the cheap seats.

  Somewhere in the middle of a question about Genghis Khan, I drifted off to sleep. I slept brilliantly that night and didn't awake once until the captain came on to tell us that we were beginning our decent into Lima, Peru.

    We had arrived.

Chapter Three

Lima

It was 2 a.m. in Lima when we landed, it was dark out, yet I didn't need my eyes to detect that I was in a strange land. The air was the dead give away that I was no longer in Salt Lake City. The air back home was distinctly dry, this was humid much like the air in Atlanta, a significant difference being that I could taste it. It tasted like car exhaust and when I first got there I just thought it was from being on an airport runway, not true. The environmental controls in Peru (as in much of the third world

I would later discover) were severely lacking. This didn't get me down however, I smiled broadly and inhaled a big breath of that nasty metropolitan air and stomped my feet on the tarmac. I was twenty five years old and this was the first time my feet had felt the earth of an entirely different continent. It was invigorating, for once in my life I had thrown caution to the wind and challenged myself to explore the unknown of a completely foreign culture and land. Yes, I believed at that moment JD and I were prepared for the adventure of a life time. What I didn't know at the time was that adventure certainly awaited us, but the word "prepared" would not have been the greatest of adjectives to describe our state of being in relation to what lay before us.

      I looked around at all of the commotion of an international airport; jets were taxiing here and there, baggage throwers unloading luggage, that cute flight attendant Katie was directing traffic and wishing everyone a goodbye. I may be mistaken, but to this day, I swear that she slipped JD her phone number. We entered the airport and waited patiently to get our luggage. I was torn between being elated at the opportunity to explore and the exhaustion that I felt from having traveled for twenty-four hours. After little debate, our curiosity gave way to our need for a warm bed. We had decided to just go directly to the "Rodriguez Family youth hostel". It was a place that had been recommended as a friendly accommodation on the North side of Lima by our guide book. We changed some of our money for the local stuff, which in Peru is the Sole. At the time the exchange rate was over three to one. We went instantly from middle class schmucks in America, to rich travelers in Peru. We were met by a crowd of people the moment that we left the doors of the airport.

It was a very busy scene for being in the wee hours of the morning. I briefly felt like one of the Beatles, before I realized these were not adoring fans, but taxi drivers looking for some customers. We took the very first taxi driver who came to us; a young guy named Pablo who really didn't speak English, but fortunately for us JD spoke enough Spanish to get by. We told him the address that we were trying to get to and he quickly asserted that we did not want to stay in that neighborhood. He said that it was very dangerous and that his friend owned a hotel that was very nice. JD assured me that this was just a scam that the cabbies used to throw business to certain hotels in exchange for kickbacks. I had no experience with it either way, so I trusted JD and we convinced Pablo that we did want to go to the address that we specified, but thanked him for his suggestion.

He shrugged his shoulders and reluctantly agreed.

Previous to this excursion, I had only left the country one other time and that was a trip to Tijuana, Mexico. One spring break in college, ended up drunk and wandering Revolution Street following my friend Carter while he tried hitting up every pharmacy for drugs you couldn't buy in the US and searching for the infamous donkey-show. Fortunately we found neither. It wasn't a great time, but it did give me a point of reference.

My eyes first gazed upon the streets of Lima and in my travel-stupor it looked just like Tijuana. The sidewalks were dirty, with trash strewn here and there; graffiti marred the surface of old buildings and stop lights. As we raced down the crowded streets of Lima, I subconsciously reached for the seatbelt that I knew wasn't there. I just had to make sure that it wasn't. The taxi that we were driving in wasn't really a taxi like one may come to consider in the States. In Peru, as is the case in much of the world, if you own a car you're a taxi driver; there's no meter and all of the payments are arbitrary and argued upfront. We were paying 40 Soles to get to our hostel, which both of us agreed was too much, but we were too tired to argue really. No, this was not a typical cab you might find in New York or Chicago, though ironically regardless of where you are the cabbies are never American.

 Anyway, as I was saying there was no seatbelt in this car and at that moment in time I would have felt a lot better about things had there been one. As far as I could tell, all of the traffic laws in Peru seemed to be merely suggestions, suggestions that the local drivers didn't seem to care much for. The horn was used by our cabby in place of the brakes.

Instead of slowing down when things got a little tight, he would just honk his horn to let people know to get out of the way because he was not stopping. We didn't stop at any signs we passed along the way, that was until we nearly broadsided a bus that had stalled in an intersection. While our cabbie rolled down the window to let the bus driver know what he thought, I took the time to let my blood pressure relax a bit and gaze out my window.

The sight to the passenger side of the vehicle was two grown men rolling on the ground beating the shit out of each other, on older woman who could have passed for a prostitute screamed at them in Spanish, while others around her pretended not to notice. Not caring for the sight to the right of our car my eyes darted to the driver's side. There was a garbage can on the corner. Based on the garbage around the can, I decided that not littering in this town was again only a suggestion. A homeless man who had had too much to drink was taking advantage of it as he vomited profusely into it. I looked up at JD, who just smiled and shrugged his shoulders. Growing up in Harlem had introduced him to experiences similar to this. This may have been a common scene, for a common street, on a common night in Lima, but it was certainly a sight to behold for a sheltered boy from Salt Lake City. As it turns out I really didn't know very much at all about the world and that would become more than apparent as this trip wore on.

    There may be a lot of scam artists in this world, but our cabbie was not one of them. JD and I were dropped off on the corner of an all dark street, full of homeless people and thugs. Yup, we had thought that the guy had just been trying get us to go to his buddy's hostel, as it was, he was just sincerely trying to keep us from staying in what appeared to be the Lima equivalent of Compton. I expected a Peruvian-Ice Cube to round the corner at any minute, not the cute family feature film Ice-Cube of today, but the menacing-thug Ice-Cube of NWA. Anyway, JD and I decided not to spend too much time hanging on the corner and instead made our way inside the hostel, which really didn't look like much, just a giant locked gate leading to a dark stairwell. There was an intercom. We rang it and were quickly buzzed up.

    The Rodriguez Family Hostel was actually a bit more friendly looking on the inside. It kind of made you forget the urban war zone that was the world down below. Senora Rodriguez was a friendly woman in her fifties; she showed us around and led us to our rooms, she spoke quickly and much of that was completely foreign to me. I was wishing I had paid better attention in Spanish class all those years ago. My Spanish teacher was a cute little Mexican woman named Senorita Vasquez and she always wore these summer dresses that revealed a bit too much cleavage when she bent over to help someone. Hardly fair to expect a 17-year-old to learn anything with the constant distraction of a sassy 25-year-old Spanish teacher playing show and tell all day.

    As I was saying, Senora Rodriguez showed us to our room, it was full of bunk beds, a few of which were already occupied by bodies that stirred slightly as we entered. We thanked her again and promptly went to bed. Despite being amazingly tired I did not sleep all that well, the window high up on the wall was open, which was great to bring some air into our room, but with no screen it also let in mosquitos, so I slept most of the night with my head below the covers. It made it hard to breath, but I managed. The night wasn't nearly long enough, I awoke as other occupants of the room were starting to get ready for the day. JD and I had paid 6 dollars between the two of us for this room, a great deal for a place to sleep, but as I was waking to my first morning in the southern hemisphere, I was thinking that it may be worth it to spring for our own room next time.

  By the time I got up, JD had already left. From what I gathered from Senora Rodriguez he would be back soon from wherever he had gone and that breakfast was ready when I wanted it. I wandered to the dining area where my breakfast was waiting for me. A typical Peruvian breakfast is this sort of dry toast stuff with marmalade and instant coffee. I'm not a coffee snob, so I actually rather enjoyed it and I was very hungry. The last thing that I had had to eat was a bottle of wine on the plane and that seemed like ages ago.

The table in the dining area was not empty. When I got there, I was met face to face with two very beautiful young women, more travelers by the looks of them and in no way did they look as if they belonged to the rugged streets down below. I was curious to speak with them, but without JD to strike up a conversation with strangers, I was pretty much useless. I nibbled on my toast and smiled politely at my two table guests. Eventually the brunette (the other being a very pretty blonde) turned to me and offered a polite:

"Buenos dias."

"Buenos dias." I quickly responded. Unfortunately that was the best Spanish that I knew.

She continued to ask me questions about my name and where I was going. We struggled to speak to one another for quite some time, with the sexy blonde chiming in once and a while. After about twenty minutes, she turned to me and said,

"Do you speak English?"

"Si...I mean yes." I responded. "Very well actually".

"Oh thank god." She said in a very friendly French accent.

"My English is much better than my Spanish."

Funny, it had only been a day, but already it was nice to be speaking some English. Her name was Michele and her friend's name was Amelie. Amelie didn't speak any English, so she just stayed in the corner and looked pretty and picked at her breakfast occasionally, without really eating much of it. Apparently she was enjoying that dry toast just as much as I was. Michelle on the other hand proved to be very talkative and very interested in me. She had never been to America and had a lot of questions about it. She was an art student on break from college in Paris. I thought that she was really smart and knew a lot about America for having never been there. I would find out later that almost everyone in the world knows something about America and everyone has an opinion about the place. Some of them true, some of them not.

We finished up our breakfast and they left for the day, Michelle said that they were going to stay the next night in the tourist district of Mira Florez and said they were going out for drinks at a bar called El Toro Negro. I told her that I would try to meet them there. Soon they were off and I returned to my room in the best mood that I had been in as long as I could remember. I discovered JD had returned and was packing some groceries into his backpack.

I told him the news about the two French girls. He was elated. It would work out just perfectly as we had only planned to spend one day in Lima anyway. According to him we could meet these French girls, get drunk and laid, crash at their place, save a few bucks on the hostel and then jump on a bus to the mountain town of Huaraz. Supposedly they had some wicked back-packing in that area. But for now we were off to paint the town red.

Chapter Four

Mira Florez

Mira Florez is the nicest area in Lima, full of gift shops and coffee houses, cafes and bars. It's generally the safest place in town and where our cabbie last night was so kindly trying to steer us. The sun was trying its best to show its face through the ubiquitous blanket of smog that crowned the Lima skyline, the streets were bustling and JD was arguing with a street vendor over the price of a wood carving of Machu Pichu. I couldn't understand much of it, but the local guy didn't seem to be budging much on his price. After an eternity JD turned to me.

"Lets get out of here or we're gonna miss the girls"

"The problem is these people are poor but not starving," I assured him.

It was true. The people here were, if anything, a bit on the chubby side. After being there for a bit I began to understand why. The people of Peru value their leisure time quite a bit and something deep fried is always a popular item on the menu. Starving, desperate people were much easier to barter with. It wasn't a ploy here, they really didn't care if you bought their item or not. We just stopped trying after a while. Third world one, clueless American travelers zero.

We made our way down the streets of a nice neighborhood. The homes were mostly surrounded by very high walls with that Spanish decor of broken bottles cemented in the top to threaten the most brazen of thieves. I could see this being a problem here, the homes were so much larger then the nasty apartment high rises that surrounded the Rodriguez Family Hostel. The walls weren't the only things keeping people from robbing the riches of the Lima elite, AK-47's did the trick too. You'd catch security guards wandering the premises, they looked bored. I bet they didn't see much action. I wouldn't try anything, they looked bored but capable. The security guards weren't the only ones with AK's in Lima, the *Policia* had them too and they were all over. A cordial bunch though, we got lost a couple of times and these friendly assault rifle-toting, direction-giving brothers were always very helpful. I really couldn't imagine a more stark contrast than that of my experience with the cops back home and I was white. Don't even get JD started on it.

Once when we were in college, JD had rented a house with a bunch of other guys, friends of his and they were all black, except Greg Stamatakis, who was Greek-Mexican I think. Anyway, he and all the roommates used to get together on Wednesday nights and play Trivial Pursuit. JD was damn good too, he knew all kinds of trivial information. That night I told JD I'd stop by after work. When they'd been playing about an hour, there was a knock at the door. JD answered the door thinking it's me and to his surprise no one's there. Thinking it was just some kids messing around he goes to close the door when a cop forces it back open and demands to know where the "minors" were. I guess one of the neighbors was scared of the house full of young black guys (and Greg) and had called the police because they thought they were having a party or something. JD was only twenty at the time, so he was a minor himself. His retort to the dim-witted cop was, "How old do you have to be to play trivial pursuit?" About this time I arrived on the scene, I see this little white cop, yelling at JD.

"What seems to be the problem officer?" I say with genuine concern.

I must have startled that paranoid son of a bitch because his reaction was to night stick me in the sternum and toss me next to JD on the front porch. God that hurt! I still remember the pain vividly. This cop then tells us that he's shutting the party down and that everyone needs to go home. By this point all of JD's roommates had put the game on hold and made their way to the front door to see what all the fuss was about and the cop's partner, a young woman who looked like a man and was about cop #1's same height (Roughly that of an oompa loompa), rounded the corner of the house with her hand resting on the handle of her gun, ready to draw. The first cop yelled at us all one more time to get out of here and that he was shutting this party down. Again, JD tried to reason with the guy by letting him know that not only is there no party, but also that he has no place to go because this was his home. The cop who had stopped listening long ago, screamed one last time "Vacate the premises now!" His hand went to his belt, time seemed to slow down, I was hunched over in pain nursing my recently bruised sternum and trying to catch my breath, I could hear my heart and I swear it skipped about three beats while this munchkin's hand went to his hip to draw a weapon. I thought for certain that this guy was going to shoot us. To my delight it was only pepper spray. I say this in the most facetious of tones, yes it was great that this guy didn't riddle my friend with bullets, but anyone who's ever been pepper sprayed can account for the sizable pain that is going to accompany your next fifteen minutes of life. JD's next fifteen minutes were even worse, while I nursed my sternum and tried to grasp what had just happened and the lady cop who looked a bit like a petite Pete Rose held the rest of JD's roommates at bay with her 9 mm, the oompa loompa proceeded to kick JD while he was on the ground gasping for breath as his skin, eyes and lungs felt the burn of concentrated chi-an pepper. That little guy gave JD a beat down like I didn't think I'd ever see. They cuffed him and took him to jail and left the rest of us behind.

 Greg and I went down and bailed him out. We left the rest of the boys at home thinking that they would make an already volatile situation worse. No charges were ever filed against JD, the lack of evidence against him being indicative of the fact that he hadn't in any way broken any laws. I ended up talking to some internal affairs guys at the police department hoping that I could testify and press charges against the cops and at least get them fired. The guys that I talked to were cordial, but assured me that without a witness who wasn't involved, it would just be our story against theirs and that I would never win, so to just let it go. I considered briefly getting a lawyer and fighting it. That only lasted long enough for me to actually look up how much it costs per hour for a lawyer's services. As it turns out normal people can't afford justice. They stopped playing Trivial Pursuit after that. It all went away, my and JD's bruises healed, but I don't believe that JD's ego ever did and for me....well a little piece of my faith in our system died that night too. Yeah, the cops down here were a lot nicer.

We ended up finding those girls surrounded by locals at the El Toro Negro Bar. They seemed to be enjoying the attention they were getting, but quickly lost interest once we arrived. We all got a table together and ordered a round of drinks. JD's Spanish was pretty good, but he spoke some broken French too and the girls loved him for it, they were a little drunk when we got there and we caught up quickly. The drinks were so cheap we just kept the shots coming all night. It was a great time and things started to get a little wild, it all gets a little blurry, but I remember a lot of laughing and some body shots, somehow we ended up back at their place and well, long story short, JD ended up sleeping with both of them....yeah I know, I thought that story would end better too. In any case we awoke the next morning said goodbye, exchanged contacts and then JD and I were off to challenge the peaks of the Peruvian Andes!

Chapter Five

The "Poor" Plan

The following morning we caught a bus from Lima to a town called Huaraz, where there was supposed to be some great backpacking according to our guide book. The buses here were a lot more modern than I expected. You always see these old buses of South America in the movies, that are crowded, dirty and usually have a goat tied to the roof. This one was very modern and clean; there was even a television for movies...there was also a goat tied to the roof.

As we departed Lima, my eyes were drawn to the view out of my window. Surrounding Lima proper, for miles in every direction were, well I guess you would call them suburbs. This area had dirt roads, with the occasional unfinished apartment building and mud brick dwellings with tin roofs and windows with no glass. Clothes lines connected each of the homes with the day's laundry. At one of our stops, I saw an old woman scrubbing clothes on a wash board. I'd never seen a wash board before. Crowds of people wandered through the uneven dirt roads and foot-paths that wound through the dwellings as far as the eye could see. So this is where Lima keeps it's poor, I thought to myself. I had never seen anything like this, *real* poverty, not like America, where you were considered poor if you had the exact same things as the rich, only older and smaller. Smaller TV, smaller house, older phone, older car. No these people had almost no possessions at all. For a moment I felt incredibly ungrateful for all that I had back home.

You don't have to drive very far north of Lima, before you run into this desolate land, that our bus driver told us was the driest desert in the world. I would tend to believe him. To my right was sand, sand and more sand, I couldn't see a single living thing anywhere, no trees or bushes, not a single weed. To my left was the good ole' Pacific ocean, the sand went all the way to the water. In some sense it kind of looked like the world's biggest beach, but missing the tourists. There were no towns out here that I could see. I suppose building a city in the middle of the world's driest desert could prove to be difficult.

After a few hours, we turned East and began to climb the steep winding roads of the

Andes. Lima was at sea level and Huaraz was perched at 10,000 ft, so we had quite a climb in front of us. This was perhaps the scariest ride of my entire life. The roads are dirt and only one lane wide. There were no protective rails and those drivers went fast We meandered higher and higher up these striking cliffs, the drop from the road was often straight down for several hundred feet. From my vantage point, up on those high seats, often I couldn't see the road at all out my window, only the nausea-inducing drop to certain death. When we passed another bus, we would have to back down the road to a wider spot where they could get around us. The bus drivers, who no doubt did this every day, did this with much less care than I was comfortable with, but with the precision of a surgeon. After a while I had to stop looking out the window, it was getting dark anyway. I turned my attention to the movie that was playing. I hadn't noticed until now that it was "The Animal", a comedy starring Rob Schneider. I would find later in my travels that it was common for America to export its bad media (and its good) to the whole world and even the places that hated us, loved our movies.

I barely watched movies myself. I rarely had the patience to sit down for that long, plus, the endings to most movies seemed so predictable; in a life that's so unpredictable maybe that's what people crave. Predicability to me was boredom and boredom was death. I *needed* this trip to Peru, anything different, anything to make me feel alive.

I fell asleep half-way through the movie and when I awoke we were just arriving in Huaraz. JD led us down the streets of this little mountain town to our hostel. I slept great that night for the first time in a while. I awoke in the morning and I *mean* early, to the sounds of a rooster's crowing. We were right downtown, I couldn't imagine where they were keeping roosters this close to my room. Never the less I woke up early and went for a walk around town. JD slept in, that guy could sleep through anything, he was probably exhausted from the night before, bastard. I stopped at a small coffee shop and helped myself to that ever present dry-bread stuff they ate here, with some marmalade and a cup of instant coffee. While I was sitting out front of the café, enjoying the brisk spring air, (though it was fall down here I kept forgetting) a young boy approached me about buying a postcard or some gum. I bought two postcards and a box of Chiclets. He seemed to be delighted by this magnificent transaction, he smiled, thanked me and was on his way. The sun was just rising above the snow-capped peaks that surrounded this city on all sides. It was like a fortress with a wall of mountains in 360' degrees, the peaks like watch towers. I have to say it's one of the prettiest cities I've been to and certainly the prettiest that I had seen at this time.

    I met up with JD a while later and we looked up a guide for mountaineering. These places were quite common in Huaraz. It was home to world class backpacking and ice-climbing. We found a guide, his name was Alex, a good looking, active type of guy and as luck would have it, he was American. It was nice to speak English and it eased the information gathering for our trip. He was about thirty years old I would guess and ran the business with his girl friend, who was Chilean but spoke impeccable English. He was curious how things were going back in the States, as he hadn't been home in five years. Funny that he still called it home, he didn't seem to have much desire to return and told us that when he was tired of

Huaraz, he was probably moving to Santiago, that's where his girlfriend was from. We asked Alex if he knew of any cool hikes that weren't hot tourist spots. We told him we were looking to avoid crowds and find some adventure.

He took out a giant map of the area and pointed us towards a canyon that he said he'd been meaning to explore, but never had the chance. He explained to us that on the other side of the mountain range was a little village called Chavin, where we could catch a bus back to Huaraz if we could get to it. He said he was pretty sure that the canyon connected to this village.

    I started getting very excited at this point, this seemed like the perfect adventure, no guided tour, no sherpas packing all of your gear. Just me and my boy going out to conquer nature. Alex wasn't going to guide us, because he was already busy with a guided trip for some ice climbers for the next week. He said that he had room in his van however and that he would let us tag along and drop us off at the mouth of the canyon and all we had to do was pitch in for gas. It sounded fantastic.

We spent the day gathering supplies, buying food and water, we had brought a water filter from home and JD had brought a gas stove that could run off of normal gasoline. We stopped and filled it with some "Petro" at the gas station, that also sold some local liquor called Pisco. It was heavy, but JD didn't think that we could go a week without a little something to warm our bellies, I couldn't disagree.

    I awoke again to my roosters, which was fine, because Alex was planning to leave before sunrise and he was right on time. I couldn't have been happier. It felt like something out of a movie, I wasn't sure where I was going, and I hadn't even given a thought to my job or any of my problems back home. JD and I shared the van with four other guys, who were going with Alex on an ice-climbing trek. Ice-climbers are an adventurous sort of people and this bunch in particular was quite eclectic. There were two Columbians, Mateo and Diego, they were about my age and spoke English with barely an accent, when I pried, it seemed that they were both rich kids from Bogota who had gone to college at Stanford in the U.S. They had recently graduated and were just playing for a while before they went to Law school. Then there was Mohammad, an Egyptian kid who had traveled the world over, climbing every mountain that he could. He loved to travel and loved to climb and probably would have talked to me about it all day. He said that he loved meeting new people and espoused his belief that everywhere you go, people were just people and it was governments that convinced us all that we were very different. He thought it funny that he was commonly mistaken for an Israeli.

"We look the exact same!" He said with a laugh.

And yet he couldn't understand why their countries hated each other so much. He said that travel is what makes you tolerant of others and that everyone should travel if they can.

This is when the American chimed in. His name was Jim, he had long hair and a huge beard and looked as if he'd been living outdoors for a year. In fact he had.

Jim had landed his dream job a year ago. He got to walk the worlds hiking trails and write a book about it. In the last year, he had been to every continent, hiking the Himalayas, Mount Kilimanjaro, the Alps, his list went on and on.

This was his last stop before he went back to the U.S. to complete the book by walking the trails of America. He seemed a little sad by this admission, like the adventure of a life time was coming to an end.

Between these four adventurers, I believe that they had been to every country in the world. It was very informative, they each took turns professing to us, what country had the most beautiful women in the world. It would go something like this "The French women are incredible man it doesn't get any better than that" or "Oh man, you haven't seen anything until you've been to Ethiopia", "No way, Columbia...." And on and on this went for what seemed to me a comical amount of time. The only thing I was able to gather was that there were beautiful women all over this planet and that is something that I would find first hand to be true a bit later in this story.

This motley crew of world-traveling ice-climbers, thought that we were crazy when our guide Alex pulled the van over in the most remote region of the Andes, on a dirt road in the middle of nowhere. He let us out and pointed in the general direction of where he *thought* would take us to a village in about a week and then drove off, leaving nothing but silence and a dust trail behind him. In retrospect the concern of these well traveled thrill seekers may have been something for us to pay attention to. We did not.

    There we were, JD and me and the mountains. Three days ago we were in an airport in Atlanta, twenty four hours ago we were at sea level in Lima, now we were facing a menacing trek through the Andes beginning in a valley at twelve thousand feet above the ocean. We were above the tree line so these striking, jagged mountains were covered only with wild grasses and weeds and the occasional giant cactus. The cactus were huge, sometimes fifteen feet tall, but it seemed even they weren't very happy being up this high, with so little oxygen around. As we climbed the mountain the cacti became more and more sparse and once we set up camp for the night, we couldn't see any at all. I'd never seen mountains like this, no trees, bushes, nothing. Just grass and rocks.

 The canyon we were in was incredibly steep and finding level ground that first night proved to be impossible. Finally after we were too exhausted to go any further and the sun began to set, we chose a spot that was the best we could do, but it was not level and it was full of rocks. It didn't make for a terribly comfortable sleep. In fact I don't believe I slept much at all that first night. It was much colder than I anticipated as well. Again, I had forgotten that this was Peruvian fall and not our spring. All I brought was a sweater and a rain jacket.

The nights were long, we were relatively close to the equator which this time of year gave us about twelve hours of day and twelve hours of night. It was too cold at night to spend a lot of time outside of the tent and because we were above the tree line there was no firewood anywhere. When the sun went down, we soon got into our tent for the next twelve hours, whether we were tired or not. That first day, I really was tired. We went to bed without cooking any dinner, as neither of us felt like it. Tired of trying to sleep, I got out of my tent in the middle of the night and took a look around. A cold wind had started blowing down the canyon, I held my arms to my body for warmth. There was no moon out and the canyon was domed by a cloudless sky. I could see the stars clearly, it was beautiful. I had never seen the stars of the southern hemisphere and had forgotten that they were different down here.

Sure enough I looked for Orion and the Big Dipper, anything that I was familiar with...nothing. It was breathtaking, the stars were so bright that they painted the canyon walls in that surreal starlight, I felt like I was on another planet. From my camp-site I could see for miles the way that we had come and for miles up the canyon where we were going. I laughed to myself. It suddenly struck me as funny that only humans would be silly enough to leave their warm comfortable beds and homes where food, shelter, entertainment and safety were readily available, to travel half-way around the world where they had none of this. Then the reason seemed obvious, as I stood alone on that ledge, the only sound, a subtle breeze blowing down the canyon, the air crisp and clean, the giant, snow capped peaks surrounding me on all sides, bathed in the starlight. This was amazing! I stood there enduring the cold for a long time, I cleared my mind of thought and just absorbed the sensation of being alive.

After those long, mostly sleepless twelve hours, the sun came up. I got out of my tent and found JD sipping some tea and watching the sunrise. I joined him; the conversation between us was light as we were both still really tired. The tea tasted fantastic and warmed my whole body, I drank it quickly...and seemingly just as quickly, vomited. At the time I thought that my empty stomach just couldn't handle the caffeine. I would find though that what I was experiencing was just the beginnings of altitude sickness.

We climbed higher and higher into the Andes and our pace became slower and slower. As we climbed in altitude our lungs were struggling to find the ever- diminishing air. I sympathize with smokers and emphysema patients; this must be what they feel like every day of their lives, like there's a giant anvil sitting on your chest and your boots feel as if they're made of lead.

    The scenery continued to amaze me, we spent a good mile climbing land that was the victim of glacial retreat. The topsoil had been torn away by the giant mass of ice, leaving nothing for plant life to grow. The result was a barren landscape of gray and black rock as far as I could see. It was eerie and lifeless like the surface of the moon. Much like the moon, *I* was feeling more and more lifeless as the day carried on. It was maybe three clock when I convinced JD to stop for the day. I struggled to set up camp, as I was feeling awful. I threw up again, multiple times and was beginning to be very concerned. We were days from any kind of help, medical or otherwise. My illness was getting worse and an early winter storm appeared to be on the rise.

I must have looked like a ghost, because JD wouldn't hear any arguments about me helping him find firewood. He set off to find some fuel for our fire and I stayed back at my tent. I finally found the sleep that I had missed the last two days. It was fleeting however, I was awoken by JD with the news that there was no firewood anywhere near our camp. We were far above the tree line now. There was nothing but small sticks and grass, nothing that would provide us with heat and the snow began to fall.

I was a pessimist by nature, but JD was not. He was an optimist, always. Sometimes I thought he was foolish for being so, other times I admired him for it. He was always bringing me up when I was down, telling me that everything was gonna be okay. But this night, no reassurance came. He sat next to me on a rock, huddled over and shivering and for the very first time, I saw fear in his eyes. I shared that fear, it was hard to deny that we were in some serious trouble.

    Without fire, dinner was just some trail mix and a granola bar. Feeling exhausted and freezing, both of us went to bed early, but I stayed awake for hours. My mind raced and my anxiety built. I thought about my parents and how they loved me, even though I gave nothing back to them. I thought about how I might never see them again. The temperature continued to drop and my fingers and toes began to ache. This trip to Peru was the biggest risk I'd ever taken. The closest thing to an adventure I'd ever had and now I wasn't sure that I would ever be able to share it with anyone. The snow was falling faster and faster by the minute and the wind began to blow, soft at first. The barely-audible whistle down the canyon soon turned into a deep moan and began to rattle the tent. I had nothing but my cheap sleeping bag to keep me warm. I hadn't even brought a coat! We were a couple of stupid Americans in way over our heads. I was in the Andes for Christ's sake! These were some of the largest mountains in the world, we were over 16,000 feet of elevation. How could I not think it would be cold? My teeth began to chatter and my feet went from feeling numb to feeling like they were on fire. Now I was wishing the numbness would return. It didn't, instead radiating pain from my fingers to my toes. My entire body convulsed with shivers as my muscles tried desperately to provide my body with warmth. I know everyone finds themselves in trouble from time to time. I've certainly had my share, but nothing like this. I always held out hope that I could get through almost anything, but as my mysterious illness worsened and the storm grew my hope was actually gone.

I was preoccupied with death, I thought about it constantly. What kind of man would I be? How would I react? This wasn't what I expected. I was filled with this hollow feeling of hopelessness. I was scared, more scared then I had ever been in my life.

What did I do when faced with death? I cried. Nothing courageous. I wasn't heroic or brave, I didn't look death in the face and laugh, I just cried and felt overwhelming fear and regret. I couldn't believe I'd ever considered killing myself. When really faced with the end of my life, I couldn't think of anything that I wanted more than to live. Just to see tomorrow, to see my mother again, to feel warm again. I made a promise to myself that night, if I survive this, if I found a way to get home, things were going to change. It wasn't just going back to that stupid job parking cars for rich people, that life of no motivation, no ambition, no search for change, that life of self-loathing. No, things were going to be different from now on! Somewhere in my feverish thoughts and sobbing, something magical happened...I accepted it. I was going to die, maybe this very night, but either way it was inevitable. How simple. In the heart of that vicious storm, even with freezing pain radiating through my body, consciousness faded away. I went to sleep, not certain if I would ever wake...To my surprise, I did.

    I awoke the next morning to the sun shining, it was glistening off of the six inches of new snow surrounding my tent. JD was screaming at the canyon
"Is that all you got!"
    I joined him, he turned to me and smiled but didn't say a word. I knew exactly

what he was feeling and exactly what he was thinking. We were going to make it.

The storm had subsided during the night and miraculously I was feeling better. It wasn't actually a miracle, your body just needs time to adjust to the lack of oxygen. It made sense, how else did the locals live here all year long? We made it to the village of Chavin, I found the best, most expensive hostel they had and it cost me seven dollars. The moment I got to my room, I collapsed into my bed. I slept like I had never slept before. I didn't toss and turn, never got up for a drink, I literally just slept for 15 straight hours. I caught a bus back to Lima the next day and from there a flight back to Salt Lake City. JD stayed behind, he was determined to see the ruins of Machu Picchu. He said, he'd never be this close again. I couldn't argue with him, but I was ready to go home. I was going to change my life and I wanted my new life to start as soon as possible. I felt as though I had a second chance and I was determined to make my life an incredible one!

Chapter Six

Progress Takes Time

    The dark clouds above were threatening rain. You become very observant of the weather when you work outdoors. I was a blue collar stiff, a working man, not a hard working man mind you but a working man all the same. I was the lowest of the low, a valet. I parked cars for rich people outside of Farlaino's Italian restaurant...Oh god! I've told this story before! (Sigh) Well, the truth was, I was back home and seemingly nothing had changed. I was still working the same shitty job parking cars, the umbrella was still broken, and yes, it had just begun to rain. In spite of my boss's instruction to stay next to the booth I was leaning against the building under the awning to get out of the weather. I opened up my book and began to read. It was Plato's Republic; sounds a bit pretentious I know. Reading this book in public looks like you're trying too hard to be intellectual, but I really liked it. Come on it's Plato, the brother must've had something good to say to achieve this kind of longevity. I fantasized when I read these books that I was one of them, one of the great skeptics like Voltaire or Rouseau. Maybe I could be?

So this was my new passion. I was a philosopher! (Or so I deemed myself) This was how I'd justified making no obvious changes in my life. I took turns reading all those books that you may or may not have read but were definitely a fixture on your bookshelf in college:

"On The Road", "A Catcher In The Rye", "Heart of Darkness". I'd catch myself trying to engage in interesting conversation with customers who would come to my restaurant. I'd sneak questions into the transaction like "Who defines morality?" or "What is the nature of consciousness?" On this particular day, the customer whom I was speaking to was a regular. I didn't know his name, but he was this big black dude with a platinum grill. He wore lots of jewelry and drove a shiny new Cadillac Escalade with tinted windows.

"I hear what you're saying, but if Kant was an Audi A4, then certainly Aristotle was a Cadillac." I said.

"Get me my damn car, right now!"

He said in a tone that led me to believe he may do more than just alert the manager. This is how most people responded to my political and philosophical platitudes. I understand now that I was just bothering them. They wanted food, they weren't looking for a preacher. I was just a bumper sticker shouting at them as they tried to enjoy themselves. They didn't want to exchange ideas. Who was *I* anyway? To them just an annoying servant who never retrieved their car fast enough.

I finished my shift that night and went home to find that the power had been shut off. Oh that's right... I remember now. The many notices I had received about how I should pay my power bill. It's a hard life being a philosopher, the only thing worse than the pay are the benefits. It was pitch black in the apartment, but I knew the dimensions like the back of my hand. I found my way to the couch and slumped down into it. I sighed, another long day. I sat in the dark and quietly contemplated my life and my choices. I fought off questions creeping into my mind, questions about who I was and where I was going, these kinds of thoughts never made me happy. Does it always have to follow suit that self-awareness leads to self consciousness?

That cute couple above me were having loud and what sounded like fantastic sex. Did they ever stop? Sometimes I thought it was hot, right now I just found it really, really depressing. I was alone, I was always alone. I tried to make friends, to be friendly and treat people right, but I didn't always know what to say. I found people interesting, I would listen to their stories, I thought I was a good listener. In spite of all I thought I had to offer, it seemed most people didn't care whether I was around...A problem for another day I suppose.

It occurred to me that I was hungry, I stumbled into the kitchen and used the light from my cell to look through my cupboards, Mac and Cheese, Top Ramen, both of those require electricity to cook. I was too tired to go anywhere, so I just sat there and felt hungry, lonely, depressed, sorry for myself and a whole bunch of other adjectives describing a pitiful, pitiful human being.

I started to cry.

The phone rang.

Instinctively, I answered it, even though I was in no mood to speak with anyone. It was my mom, oh god, of all the people I didn't want to talk to right now.

"Hi, Mom?"

...

"What? No, no I haven't been crying. I just have allergies. No really Mom it's just allergies, it's fine."

...

"I know you're worried about me Mom, but please don't. I'm working on it and I'm going to get a new job. It just takes time. It's a bad economy and you know, things like that."

"Look Mom you caught me at a bad time, can I call you back? No really, I was just about to head over to JD's. Yeah, yeah. We're going to a movie. I don't know. Some action movie that JD wanted to see. Yes, yes I will call you later okay. I love you too bye."

I had hidden my tears, as best I could, but after that phone call I felt even worse. I just wanted to be happy, I wanted something to do with my life that seemed worthwhile. I simply wanted a change for the better and I didn't know how to make that happen, I racked my brains every day only to come up empty. My life was like that dream where you just can't run fast enough to get where you're going, like running in a pool and every time you look up you're no closer to where you want to be.

There was always a part of me that felt I could do better, if I just tried, if I just wanted it bad enough. Life was a puzzle, a Rubik's cube. It was difficult, but it was do-able. I watched a girl do it in 30 seconds once (the Rubik's cube that is), there must've been a trick to it. There must be a trick to life too, because how else was I supposed to survive it? If I didn't feel like it could be better, I would've ended it all long ago. People who don't suffer depression don't really understand this sick feeling that you have all day, this emptiness in the pit of your stomach that no food or drink can ever fill. There's nothing observably wrong with you and it is indiscriminate, it hits the rich, the poor, successful people and failures like me.

    I drifted off to sleep on the couch, awaking only to the alarm alerting me that it was time to go back to my lousy job, for another day in my fantastically-uninspiring life.

Chapter Seven

Two Dead Gangsters And The Opportunity Of A Lifetime

It was a nice night here at Farlaino's, a warm breeze drifted through the air. It felt good, I enjoyed the warm summer nights here in Salt Lake, they made my job just a bit more bearable. I was closing tonight and I was working alone, it was near midnight and very quiet downtown, I think that everyone had left the restaurant. I still had a couple of cars left in the lot, I wonder where the owners were at? The jerks had probably gone to the bar or something. I was used to staying late, this was actually my favorite time of day, when everything slowed down. I was finishing a double shift and I was exhausted. That's the price you have to pay if you want your electricity turned back on. Aside from being very tired, I felt good. Nothing had changed, really, but something was about to...

I closed the book I'd been reading and sat it down. I opened up my lock box, one set of keys left. I checked my watch: 1:08 AM. The restaurant had been closed for a while, so they must have gone to the bar. This happened a lot actually and you just had to wait for them. I was really starting to get tired now, even though I wasn't that excited to go home, because my power was still off. I glanced around the empty streets, a homeless guy strolled past pushing a shopping cart. He didn't ask for money, just gave me a friendly nod. Once he'd rounded the corner I kind of wished I had given him some money...the sound of firecrackers interrupted my thoughts and broke the silence of the night. It seemed a bit out of place, and caught me off guard. My mind naturally attempted to explain the noise... the Fourth of July? No. A sporting event? To late for that. Five, six, seven more firecrackers went off in succession. Not firecrackers, gunshots! Gunshots coming from behind the restaurant. I was sure of it! Instinctively, I ran towards the gunshots, (At least instinctively for a person who doesn't care whether he lives or dies that much.) Something interesting and exciting in an otherwise dull life was going on. My heart was pounding as I sprinted back to the lot, it was empty, save for two cars. I recognized one of them as the black Escalade that belonged to my philosopher friend. The other was a lowered Honda Civic, tricked out, with expensive rims, the trunk was open. A man lay face down near the car. I knew instantly that he was dead. There was blood everywhere. I was the first one here. I approached with caution, a quick glance inside the Civic's trunk revealed bags of what looked like drugs, I couldn't really tell what kind as they were wrapped and taped into bricks. I walked around to the back to the Escalade parked just a few feet away, the back was open and I saw a large duffle bag inside. I stepped over the body of the philosopher who lay on the ground motionless. I reached for the bag and unzipped it slowly, my eyes locked onto what I saw inside. Cash. More money than I had ever seen, bundles and bundles of hundred dollar bills. Something stirred on the ground next to me, I spun around to see that the owner of the bag had rolled onto his stomach, he was bleeding from a huge hole in his belly, his breathing was rapid and short, he choked on his own blood. He didn't speak, but he reached for a gun lying in the blood near my feet, I hadn't noticed it before, instinctively I kicked it away. He turned his gaze back to me and looked me straight in the eyes with a frigid stare, one that made me shiver. Strangely, I still felt compelled to help him, even though he had just reached for a gun, but he was beyond help. I knew it. Sure enough, a moment later his chest stopped moving. Those creepy eyes still looked at me, but now they saw nothing. He was dead. The sound of sirens in the distance snapped me from my trance. Something took over, I was on autopilot, I grabbed that duffel bag and walked away as calmly as if I were walking in the park. As I left the scene of the crime I could hear the sirens get louder and louder until certainly they had reached the lot. By this time I was long gone. I didn't pass a single soul on the streets and only a few cars passed me on my trek back to my apartment. In retrospect, I don't know if I was in shock or what was wrong with me, but I wasn't nervous. I should have been, I just watched a man die and was now walking the streets with a ton of drug money. I didn't care if someone found me. I wasn't thinking of anything other than getting away at my own pace. The mind is as interesting as it is unpredictable, I've been nervous at every job interview I've ever had, sweaty palms, erratic heartbeat, stuttering speech and for what? A job making coffee? Parking cars? But here I was, cool as a cucumber, I walked with the confidence of a runway model all the way home.

    My apartment was pitch black, I opened the door intent on gathering a few things, but the power was still out and I could barely see inside. With a smug laugh, I shrugged my shoulders and turned right around. I left my apartment right then and there and didn't even bother to close the door, I would never set foot in there or see any of those things.

I boarded a plane that night. I paid for the ticket with cash. I even checked that duffel bag with that same relaxed demeanor. I felt so peaceful, like Buddha or like Buddha would have behaved had he just stolen a sack full of money from two dead gangsters. I was flying first class. Where was I going? Aruba. I have no idea why, I'd heard of it. It sounded exotic and there was a flight leaving that night. I sat down in my seat and stretched my legs in my oh-so spacious business-class chair. My flight attendant brought me a nightcap, the finest brandy they had. I sipped it, it tasted like the most amazing thing ever. It was sweet, with a little bit of a kick. I inhaled that incredible aroma and smiled to myself as I felt that sweet liquor warm my body. I slept like a baby on that flight. I slept without giving a single thought to the consequences of the actions I'd just taken. I really had no plans ever to return. My whole life already seemed a distant memory, a bad dream. When I awoke to the voice of the captain alerting us to our decent I felt like I was waking for the very first time.

Chapter Eight
Aruba

Upon landing in Aruba, I checked into the nicest hotel in town, "The Aruba Grande Beach Resort and Casino". It was absolutely stunning, it had the biggest fountain I had ever seen, with bronze sculptures of Pegasus dancing in the water. I was a little intimidated as I entered. The lobby was huge and a breathtaking crystal chandelier hung from the the ceiling, sculptures decorated the end tables. Everything sparkled like new. The place was buzzing with hotel help and families on vacation. I don't think anyone else really noticed how spectacular this place was; it was probably not their first time at a luxury resort. I, on the other hand, had never been in a place this fancy. I felt a bit out of place, like any minute someone would expose me as a fraud. I looked down at my clothes, I was still wearing my uniform from work. The desk clerk was friendly and didn't treat me any differently, even though I was dressed like I worked there. I checked into a suite on the top floor, it was spacious and bright, with an ocean view and a bar. This was everything I might have imagined the penthouse of the most expensive hotel in Aruba would look like. I threw my bag of money on the bed, unzipped it to grab a few dollars. I half expected it to be empty, as if I'd just dream't the whole thing. Sure enough, it was still full of money. I smiled... perfect. First things first, I asked the nice guy at the counter where I could find a good suit and he recommended a place right in the hotel. So I went exploring and found the suit shop he was talking about. "Versace" was the name on the window, I'd heard of the brand. Never in my life did I think I'd be shopping for one. I dropped a lot of money on a sensational suit, as much as I earned in two months. It felt incredible! In fact it kind of made me feel good in a way I didn't expect, already I felt a little more confident.

    I found a rental car agency that rented sports cars. After exchanging a few dollars and signing some paperwork, I found myself in this sporty little convertible Mercedes. It would do. I've driven about every car known to man and Mercedes wasn't bad, though I always thought it was not as good as Volvo, just a little sexier. I guess there's a lot in the name. Speaking of names, I needed a new one, if I was starting a new life. Something cool, something that sounded sophisticated...Andy Davis sounded like I worked at a fast food chain, picked up garbage or valet parked. No more working class name for me. I wanted something different, something with fire, something that shouted, "He must be important!"... Alas I wasn't that clever. I couldn't come up with anything at the time, so I left in search of an evening of adventure.

The sun was setting as I made my way to a nice little bar overlooking the ocean. I rolled up in my Benz, wearing my new suit, looking like a million dollars. I felt like James Bond. I was growing comfortable with this new life, and it had only been one day. I valet parked and God damn it, I tipped that son of a bitch well! I was led by a pretty hostess to my table, a spot right next to the wall that separated me from the beach below. I was just high enough I could get a great view of the sun sinking into the sea. The club was abuzz. Full of the energy and laughter that one only gets when one is a thousand miles from any of life's concerns. I had escaped to this place. I didn't care what was going to happen tomorrow, I didn't care where I had spent the last twenty-five years. I was absolutely living in the moment. It felt like karma was paying me back somehow, that I was finally being rewarded for being the "nice" guy for so long. Yes, lady Karma was looking out for me. This nice guy wasn't finishing last this time and as I would find out, she wasn't finished with me yet.

A waiter approached me and asked me in English if he could get me anything to drink. I often wondered and still do, what makes us Americans so obvious to the rest of the world. I thought for a moment, what would Bond drink? Ah yes.

"Da me un Martini, por favor". I said. The waiter seemed to respond well to me at least trying speak Spanish.

"Si, Senor".
He replied and then was off in a flash.

I would find out later that the official language of Aruba was Dutch, but most people spoke some English and Spanish and a local dialect called Papiamento. Which sounded like Spanish to me, so for the rest of my trip Instead of speaking English, I fumbled with my bad Spanish, like the novice traveler I was.

I pulled a cigar out of my jacket and clipped the end off. It was a Cuban, or at least that's what the street vendor who had sold it to me had professed. In either case I had paid thirty bucks for it and it looked nice enough. I inhaled deeply through my nose over the length of the cigar. Tobacco always smelled much better than it tasted to me. I didn't smoke, and had only ever tried a cigar a handful of times, but this seemed absolutely appropriate for where I was. I lit it up and took a long puff.

"Not bad", I thought to myself. I took a couple of drags off of that Cigar and could begin to feel myself getting a bit of a buzz from it.

The waiter returned with my drink. That was fast.

"Gracias" I said as he sat it down.

"De nada"

He was off to see to the rest of the bar. I sipped the drink and coughed, I didn't drink that much and hadn't had a martini in years. I'd forgotten that it has two components, both of which are all alcohol. It didn't taste great, but it felt like the right thing to be drinking. I scanned around the restaurant when my eyes met a woman across the bar. She was looking right at me. I first assumed that she was looking at someone behind me until I realized the only thing behind me was the Caribbean. She was a beautiful Latin girl with dark hair and bronze skin, thin, yet with curves. She wore a beach skirt and a bikini top and looked absolutely gorgeous from where I was sitting. I thought for a moment about going over to her and striking up a conversation. To my surprise, before I had the chance, she walked over to me.

"Hola" She said in a sweet and inviting voice.

"Hola" I forced out. I was intimidated by her beauty, but I don't think it was showing. She waited for more, but I couldn't think of anything to say. She beat me to the punch again.

"May I sit down?" She spoke with a thick Spanish accent.

"Certainly" So she wasn't lost. She actually wanted to sit down. This was a good start.

"Gracias"

She sat at my table and waited expectantly for me to say something. As usual, I did not. The silence didn't deter her, she smiled at my shyness and spoke.

"You are American, no?"

"No... I mean yes." I was fumbling.

I glanced down nervously and caught a glimpse of what she saw. A young American, well dressed, alone, smoking an expensive cigar and drinking a martini. A thought occurred to me: Act as she would expect you to. My confidence grew.

"What is your name?" She asked.

"Martin" There it was.

I don't know where it came from, somewhere the alter ego was sleeping deep inside me, waiting to come out. No sooner had I blurted out that name, than I became that man. The rest followed like water over a fall.

"Martin Van Sant" I repeated.

"And what is your name?"

"Anna-Maria" She extended her hand.

"Nice to meet you, Martin".

She rolled the "R" in Martin, I found the accent endearing.

"The pleasure is mine" I said.

"Are you here alone?" She inquired.

"Not at the moment" I said with a grin.

She smiled. " No, I mean are you here with anyone?"

"No".

"I didn't think so."

She was very receptive to what I was saying. I wasn't worried about what to say next or what would happen next. I just let it come to me and responded in kind. Never had I been so comfortable in my own skin, than at that moment. Though it wasn't my skin, or my words anymore. It was Martin's...but mine.

" So is it that obvious that I am an American?"

Anna-Maria nodded and smiled.

"Ah, but can you guess what state?"

Anna-maria laughed.

"By your accent?"

"Yes"

" I work at hotel and see people on holiday all the time. The other day I mistook one of my customers for an American, but he was Irish! English all sounds the same to me."

"Well you speak it very well." I complimented her.
"Thank you, I have studied very hard to learn. Where are you from?"

"Utah, ever heard of it?"
She shook her head.

"We had the Winter Olympics..."
She stared at me blankly, before smiling and adding.

"Don't feel bad, I only know like, New York, California, Texas."

She paused for a moment, then asked.

"What do you do?"

Without hesitation, I answered.

"I am a business man."

"What kind of business?"

"Finance."

"Are you here for, business or holiday?"

This was getting rough.

"What is this, twenty questions?" I said.
She didn't get the reference.

"What?"

I changed the subject.

"What do you do?" I asked.

"I work at the restaurant, in the hotel next door."

"That sounds nice, it's a pretty place to live." I suggested.

She shrugged her shoulders.

"Is ok, am working hard to save money to move to America."

"You know, it's really not that great." I warned.

"You only say that because you are from there, try living down here for a while, is much harder."

I couldn't argue with that.

"Yeah, I suppose you would know...

For a moment I became distracted by her engaging dark eyes.

"Do you want to go for a walk with me?" I asked.

Anna-Maria smiled again. What a great smile she had, I couldn't help but be drawn to it...to her.

"Yes, Martin Van Sant. I will go for a walk with you."

We left the bar and began walking on the beach, next to all of the towering hotels. The sun was nearly down now, it was only a glow on the horizon. The first stars were starting to shine, it was surreal. We walked the beach for hours, I let her tell me all about herself and she was more than willing to share. She was from Caracas, Venezuela, but both of her parents were Colombian. They had moved to Venezuela when she was just a child. She had a younger brother living in Maracaibo. He was in the merchant navy and didn't spend much time there. A friend of hers had gotten her the job at the hotel in Aruba. She was grateful for this, she made good tips from the tourists and was saving her money so that she could move to the United States and go to college. It was a dream of her parents that she would get more of an opportunity than they did. She painted America out to be this amazing place with limitless opportunity, I didn't correct her, why ruin her dream. Besides, while America wasn't perfect, it certainly had more opportunity than most of South America, as far as I knew. She wasn't really speaking of anything in particular, just her life and dreams. Which I found interesting. She was very candid, I found her voice intoxicating and her company very comfortable. Was it her making me feel this way? Hard to say, two days ago I was a valet, working in Salt Lake City. Now I was a businessman... a liar named Martin Van Sant. I was walking the beach with a beautiful girl, so intimidatingly sexy, I would've never spoken to her before today... and she approached me! Maybe it was because of my demeanor or my suit or maybe I wasn't giving her enough credit. In any case, she liked me. She was attracted to me. She laughed at my jokes, she touched me often and in very friendly ways. I knew this was going to end well. I've never just *known* that, I've hoped and usually been disappointed, but today, I knew it was different. I invited her back to my hotel and she accepted. I drove her back in that beautiful Mercedes, though she hardly seemed to notice the car. I took her back to my enormous room overlooking the ocean, again, she didn't seem to notice. Or so it appeared, it seemed that the only thing she noticed was me. We laughed and told stories, shared a bottle of wine and then we went to bed. We made love, at least it felt like love, to me. Not just sex. I was hardly the expert though, back home I had slept with two women and one of them was only one time, all collected I could count on both hands how many times I'd actually had sex. I shouldn't have felt comfortable with my abilities as a lover, but with her I did. It felt right. She responded to me with delight and made me feel incredible, I was lost in the moment and I never doubted myself. At the end of it all, she fell asleep on my chest. I spent a long time just watching her as she slept, she looked beautiful, vulnerable and innocent. She barely knew me I thought, what an amazing thing trust is. That was a night that I would never forget.

    I never even slept that evening, before the sun came up, I gathered my things and left the hotel room. I left that angel sleeping in my bed... it was all too fast. I didn't know who I was or where I was going. I'd just left my old life behind and was ready to get out and travel the world. I had a bag full of money and nothing stopping me from seeing everything I'd always wanted to see. With my bag in hand, I paused at the door and watched her. She looked lovely and sweet, I hoped that she liked me in spite of the car and the clothes, I wanted to believe that she liked me for me, but I wasn't going to find out, not this night. I had so much I wanted to do and I wanted to get started. At that moment the only thing I saw lying in bed was an anchor. What I didn't see was her waking the next morning and finding me gone. I didn't see her tears, I didn't know how bad it made her feel, so used and ashamed. I didn't see any of these things. As quickly as I entered her life I was gone. Like some kind of transient ghost or specter, I would spend the next three years of my life nearly invisible.

Chapter Nine

Traveling Man

I had been in Paris for about two weeks and I was starting to get to know the place fairly well. I spent the first week doing touristy, exploratory stuff. I went to the Eiffel Tower, The Louvre and a host of other museums. This was a beautiful city, rich with culture. Like all great cities however, Paris has a seedy side that no one likes to talk about. This is where I spent the second week. I was tracking down information. I started by asking the valets if they knew where I could score some weed.

 With enough tries and enough tips, I got where I needed to go. Not surprisingly, some of them sold weed. When I found the weed dealers, I would ask if they knew where I could find something harder, this lead me to the cocaine dealers. I loosened their lips with a few hundred dollars and got them to tell me where I could find someone who would make fake documents. It all happened really fast actually and with a fair amount of ease. I asked directly and didn't come across as nervous or cocky. I was an American, so I think most of them assumed that my being a cop was a low probability. I tossed the drugs, but kept the information which led me to one of the shadier neighborhoods I've ever been to, in *any* city. Something I didn't know even existed in Europe, but surely not in the City of Love. It was intimidating, I have to admit.

At a door in the back of a dark alley, a man stood next to a dumpster smoking a cigarette. At first it looked as though he were just holding up a wall, a waiter on break or something, but upon closer examination he had eyes like a hawk. Those eyes weren't missing anything, including me. He was a guard. He moved with the confidence of a man holding a weapon. I walked up to him slowly and said what he was waiting to hear.

"I am here to see Jean-Pierre." I said.

The man eyed me for a moment and then motioned me to follow. He said nothing, I doubt that he spoke English. I was led down a dark hallway, rooms with no doors lined the way. They had curtains strung up haphazardly revealing moments of flesh and the sounds of whispers. I think I had just stumbled into a brothel of some kind. The man I followed walked quickly and I kept pace. I wasn't terribly comfortable with where I was and wanted to get in and out of here as soon as possible. He led me to a small low-lit room in the back. A man sat on an old sofa watching TV, the show looked like some kind of French soap opera to me, but I didn't pay it too much attention. The man on the couch wore a black leather jacket, he held a cigarette in one hand and a glass of vodka in the other. He looked up at the man I had just followed in and exchanged a few words with him in French. About this time, I was really wishing I spoke French. The logical part of my brain was telling me that this guy was a businessman... a criminal too, no doubt about it, but it's bad business to kill people who can generate income. My thoughts were interrupted by the man, Jean Pierre. He spoke with a thick French accent.

"You are looking for papers, no?"

I spoke. "Yes, an American passport."

My voice did not betray my nerves. Jean-Pierre may sound like a name for some beret-wearing, crepe-eating, pussy, but this man was no pussy, he had the look of a sociopath. He was a large man and looked at me like I wasn't even human. Everything to those eyes was either a tool or an obstacle. I shuddered to think of what this man did with obstacles.

"You, American, why you need passport from me? Go to consulate. If you lose."

" I have a passport. It just has the wrong name on it."

Jean-Pierre smirked.

"What you are asking is big deal here, can land man like me in lot of trouble."

Ah, here begins the bargaining, I didn't come to bargain, he was wasting his time.

"How much?" I asked.

"Ten thousand. American." He said.

He did not have the look of a man who could be surprised easily, but I surprised him. I reached into my jacket, pulled out my wallet and counted up $10,000 in $100 bills. I handed it to him.

"When can I have it?" I said.

"Leave passport, come back, one week." He said.

I nodded.

"How do you know I wont just kill you and take what's left in your pocket?"

I answered him plainly, my voice as calm as the sea after a storm.

"I don't."

This made him laugh out loud, I knew instantly that I was in the clear.

" What is your name, my American friend with the huge balls?"

"Martin. Martin Van Sant."

"One week, Martin."

I nodded again. Jean-Pierre barked some French to the guard and he escorted me from the building.

One week later I returned to Jean-Pierre and true to his word, I had a new passport. I was now officially a new man! It was surprising to me when a criminal was true to his word. I grew up thinking that criminals were all dishonest and cutthroat and I guess that's true to some extent, but they're also businessmen. There is no regulation in this industry. If you cheat people, they don't go to the police, they go to your front door. Cheat enough people or the wrong people and you won't last long. It was supply and demand at its finest, complete free market capitalism, no tariffs or taxes, things cost what people would pay.

I left Paris that day and wouldn't return for years. My next stop was Bern. I'd heard that the Swiss bankers had started cracking down on illegal money laundering, but I found a bank willing to take a bag full of American money with no questions asked fairly easily. Yes, I had my first Swiss bank account. In no small way, I felt I had arrived. I found Bern, to be a pleasant city, but I didn't stay long, soon I was off to London, Dublin, Munich, Copenhagen, Prague and a number of small towns in between. I spent three months roaming around Europe before I headed to Asia. I went surfing in Thailand and mountaineering in Nepal.

In Tibet I met a monk who spoke English. When he found out that I was from America he preached to me the evils of materialism. He explained to me that no one in America was ever going to be happy. He said that happy people don't consume and people who don't consume wreck western economies. So in America, there are entire subjects of study dedicated to the art of self-consciousness. He called this art "marketing". He seemed to have a good point. On the other hand the life of a monk seemed quite boring to me. A lot of gardening and meditating. Would I rather be bored or unhappy? In either case I didn't stay long.

I caught dysentery in India and nearly died, I rode a bike on the Great Wall and explored the ruins of Angkor Wat. I met some of the most fascinating people I've ever encountered in Bangladesh. So poor, yet so happy. This was an obvious contradiction in my American mind. I was always taught that the acquisition of material things and a good view from on top is what brought us happiness. It didn't seem to be true for everyone. Though I wasn't quite ready to become a hippy yet, I always find that after a few months in the Third World it is nice to get back to warm showers, toilets and streetlights that work, fixed prices and roads with no potholes. Whenever the inconvenience of the poverty of the world became too much for me. I'd find myself retreating back to the first world... but never America. I wouldn't see those shores for quite some time. I grew fond of Reykjavík and Oslo. I spent nearly three months in Galway, Ireland someplace a little off the beaten path from the tourists. It was a beautiful town, the Irish always painted their houses in such bright colors, a stark contrast to their ubiquitous gray skies. I didn't mind the rain; it made everything green, plants grow and cleaned the air. The Irish were the friendliest people I'd ever run across. I'd heard Canadians were nice, yet oddly I'd never been there. The Irish were quick to buy you a beer and listen to your story or share one of their own. Everywhere I went people were curious about what was going on in the United States. Yes, in a sense, everything the United States did was big news. They determined much of what was happening around the world. The things they bought helped or hindered economies around the world. In Ireland, American tourism accounted for a huge portion of their gross domestic product...that and selling horses, who knew? And let's face it, if there's a war happening around the world, there is a good chance America's got a hand in it.

I changed so much in those years, I had learned to speak Spanish from my time in Spain, picked up a little bit of Mandarin for my time in China. I wasn't great at languages, but being surrounded by something day in and day out, forces you to use it and absorb it.

One night in Galway, I struck up a conversation with a man in a pub. O'Leary was his name. This old jovial Irish guy talked to me for hours. He was an actor by trade and flew back and forth from Galway to London quite a bit to do work playing small roles in movies and commercials. He explained to me that there were only two types of artists, "starving and compromising and he wasn't starving!" When he inquired about what I was up to and where I was from, I told him I was from the States, but that I had done quite a lot of traveling recently. He had traveled a bit himself and told me of a Greek Island that I shouldn't miss, it was called Santorini and was the most beautiful and wonderful place he'd ever been. After hearing the passion with which he described it, I knew that was where I was heading next. Life sometimes seems like a series of random events and sometimes those random events just happen to look like what you wanted to happen. I met O'Leary at this random pub in Ireland and he directed me to this island of Santorini. It was more subtle than finding the two dead gangsters and a bag full of money (That was running quite low by the way) but just as important. Many things were waiting for me in Santorini, opportunities I could not possibly have imagined. That night I got online and looked at some photos of Santorini, it looked pretty enough, I was sold. I checked out of my hotel, drove to the airport in Shannon and booked a flight that night. There was no direct flight and I had to spend a day in Lisbon, but not 48 hours from having that conversation, I found myself walking the shores of that beautiful Grecian isle.

Chapter Ten
A Playboy Is Born

I found Santorini to be everything I had imagined. It has magnificent, steep cliffs jutting out from the bluest Mediterranean water you'll ever see. The beaches are full of rough sand and small rocks. They were unlike the beaches of California or Florida, but they carried with them their own charm. Santorini was the site of an ancient volcano, a sleeping giant, one that had ended a civilization thousands of years before. They were still excavating Minoan ruins on the island. I believe those first people to settle this island must have thought that they'd stumbled onto something pretty special, I imagine life must have been a little different back then. On the other hand, when you ignored the lively cafés and motorized vehicles and just took a walk down by the sea it was easy for your mind to forget what century you lived in and just enjoy the things that had been there forever, the birds, the breeze, the rhythm of the waves crashing on the beach. I often wonder what life was like in simpler times, I wonder if there was anyone like me back then. Some young Greek, taking a bunch of drug money and settling here to find a new life. Did they even have drugs back then? I suppose there was always something to get you high and if people wanted it, then it became a commodity. Perhaps fundamentally life really isn't that different now. Back then people still stole and killed and loved and lost and had families and got divorces, there was still fidelity and infidelity, war and peace and the whole gamut.

Whatever it had been, it was now a tourist destination for Europeans. The bars and hotels were full of people from around the world. At this point traveling for me was getting to be old hat. What was most appealing about Santorini was how peaceful it was.

I checked into a hotel and made that my home for the next month. Everything was quiet and nice and made sense. I loved it here and I wanted to stay, but the truth was my money was running low and I couldn't sustain this life forever. Reality was approaching faster then I was ready.

One night I sat nursing a beer in the hotel bar. I spent almost every night at the bar and I had gotten to know the staff very well. On this particular evening, Milos, the man who ran the door, was getting into a heated discussion with a young American. I overheard the conversation.

"This club is for guests of the hotel only." Milos, repeated.

"Yes, I understand that," said the American.

"I stay here all the time, you need to understand, that my family and I bring a lot of business to this hotel and just this once I am not staying here, but I am meeting some friends later and I want to grab a drink before. It doesn't have to be a big deal"

"Is no big deal, you just must be a guest sir, check into the hotel and there will be no problems."

"Look, I've been patient, but you're starting to…"

I'm not sure why I said something. Maybe I felt sorry for the guy, or I was just excited to hear some English. As a professional traveler, I found easy conversations to be very welcome. Too often I found myself using sign language and pointing at the things I wanted.

Whatever spawned the impulse to help, this was another one of those moments that was much more important than I could have ever realized at the time.

"Oh, there you are. I got us a table, right over here." I said to the American.

"He is a friend of yours Mr. Van Sant?" Milos asked.

"Yes Milos, I'm sorry I should have told you he was meeting me."

Milos turned to the American.

"I am sorry Sir, guests of the hotel are always welcome."

"Thank you Milos and sorry for the confusion." I added, with a slip of a few bills into his hand.

"Not a problem Sir, enjoy your evening."

"You too."

I walked back to my table, the man I'd just helped followed me until the doorman was out of ear shot.

"Thanks for that, I come here all the time. I think that guy is new. Usually they just let me in."

"No problem." I said.

He extended his hand, rather formally.

"Henry Zahn, pleased to meet you."

I shook his hand, he had a firm grip.

"Martin." I replied.

"Say Martin, can I buy you a drink for helping me out."

"Sure, how about a whiskey on the rocks?"

Henry smiled.

"That's my drink, how about that. Two whiskeys over ice coming up."

A moment later Henry returned with our drinks. It turns out that Henry was quite a connoisseur of fine whiskey. This particular was Jamison, aged twelve years. He professed that while there were more expensive whiskeys Jamison was his favorite and he didn't care for the pretension. He seemed to know a lot about it, I rarely drink whiskey, but I didn't let him know this. Henry was a well-groomed, handsome guy, maybe thirty years old. He dressed in khakis and a polo shirt that looked like something you'd buy at Old Navy upon first glance. If you looked a little closer though you'd notice that this was much more fine clothing. Henry was very friendly and talkative. He had the air of a frat boy, but not one of those cocky ones, just one of those self-assured confidence of wealth kind.

"So how long have you been in Santorini?" Henry asked.

"About a month" I replied.

"And what do you think so far?"

"I think it's great."

"You know, it might be my favorite place in the whole world. A friend of mine from college came down here and bought a bar, after graduation. He lived here for about a year, I came to visit once and fell in love with the place, now I come back all the time. Is this your first visit?"

"It is."

" You should make it an annual. Where are you from?"

"Seattle." I lied.

"Seattle eh? I've seen most of the cities in the United States but not that one. Is it nice?"

"Oh, it has its charms." (I don't know why I said Seattle, I really don't know the first thing about it. Rainy weather and a fish market seem familiar, I may need to do some research, it sounds like a city Martin Van Sant should be from).

"How about yourself?" I asked.

"Oh I'm from all over, I was born in Manhattan on the upper East side and lived in Soho, Tribeca and the Village and now I have a home on Long Island. "

He said this in good humor. I laughed and played along.

"So you're from New York then?"

"Yes, that is what I'm saying, you may think of us New Yorkers as only living on our own little island and a lot of times that's true, but not me, Martin. I am a man of the world, New York is a great city, but it's not the only great city. The more places you go, the more it means when you say that it's great, I like to get around..."

Henry turned his head as he was talking to me to take notice of a nice pair of legs that led to a short skirt on a girl who just walked by.

"Like to get around, do you?"

Henry laughed.

"I suppose that statement could be true in more ways than one. I've been around the world, Martin and I tell you the most attractive women from all of Europe end up here. If I had my way. I'm not sure I'd ever leave."

"Then, you would no longer be a man of the world." I said.

"Hah, well played my friend. Say, some friends of mine are flying in tonight and we're having a party on my boat, if you don't have any plans, you should come by."

"That sounds nice Henry, I will try to make it."

"Well if you don't, enjoy the rest of your vacation. It has been a pleasure getting to talk with you Martin and thanks again for helping out with the guy at the door."

"No problem." I said.

With that, Henry finished his drink, wrote down some instructions to help me find his party, shook my hand and was gone. I went back to my room, got on my laptop and did some serious research on the city of Seattle. It was in fact a rainy city with a fish market, but I found a few more details that would help me with my ruse.

That night I followed Henry's directions to the Athinios Port. At this port was a very high-class yacht club. A man stopped and questioned me about my club status. I told him that I was meeting my friend Henry and my name was Martin Van Sant, he quickly checked the list that he had and indeed I was on it. I walked down the pier, there were beautiful sailboats and cruisers on all sides. This seemed to be where the rich of the rich went on vacation. I followed the directions to Henry's boat slip. I found his "boat" which was actually a three-hundred foot yacht. The name on the back read: "HAMPTON BEAUTY" and it was exactly that. It looked as if it were washed daily, it shined in the twilight. The Hampton Beauty had a full time staff of 17 people, a Captain and First Mate, an engineer, several deckhands, a chef, three prep cooks and two cute little servers named Alice and Betsy. Betsy also served as the boat's masseuse.

    I could see people gathering on the top deck. The party was about to begin. One of the men from the deck recognized me and called out my name, it was Henry.

"Martin, you made it!" He yelled.

"You said you had a boat, not a battleship." I replied.

"You like it? No sense in traveling the seas on an uncivilized or unfit vessel, I love this baby. Come on up, I'll give you a tour!"

My tour of the yacht began at the bottom, in engineering. Henry seemed to love this part of the ship. He introduced me to the engineer, a friendly old Filipino man named Chino. Chino had spent twenty years in the U.S. Navy and was now semi-retired working on this yacht. "She was so well built, all he had to do was watch her go." he would say. Henry had more than a passing interest in mechanics and engineering and would spend a great deal of time just watching Chino work. The ship was powered by two massive diesel engines. Chino, bragged that on calm seas she could reach 25 knots. I acted impressed, but I had no idea what a knot was. Next Henry took me to the galley, it was run by a black dude, with a large personality, who introduced himself to me as only "Chef". I'd find out later that his name was Dale and that he made some great food.

The three kitchen aides were these young Mexican guys, Pablo, Renaldo and Raul. They didn't speak much English and mostly kept to themselves. It struck me as a bit funny, that an American kitchen was still run by Mexicans, even half a world away. On that same deck, there was a fully-stocked bar and a lounge where the meals were had. The deck above held the quarters. The rooms were large and everything in them looked just like new. The Captain, a stern yet quiet man named Emile James, ran a tight ship and there was never a thing out of place or brass left unpolished. The top deck is where all of the action was happening. It was open and spacious, at the bow of the ship was another bar that seemed to be the place of congregation for this party which made sense. Alcohol was the fuel for the fire of most social gatherings. In front of the bar near the bow, there was a hot tub full of pretty people, who all knew Henry. He walked me through the crowd of these beautiful twenty-something socialites, each one greeting him with a friendly smile. He owned the ship after all and the fun they were going to have tonight would be because of him. They were polite to me and shook my hand. They didn't seem the type to be open to new people, but with Henry as my voucher, they seemed to accept me into their ranks. Henry and I walked across the deck as he gave me the lowdown on his party guests.

"I'm glad you could make it, Martin. It's always welcome to find another adventurous young American out and about."

"Thanks again for the invite, the ship is incredible." I said.

"It's actually my father's, but he only uses it once or twice a year to schmooze clients. The rest of the year, it's all mine. We used to have a smaller one, but I got caught in an unbelievable storm mid-Atlantic, somewhere between here and home, scared the hell out of me, so I traded her in for the "Beauty".

"You're a lucky man Henry, I love it already."

"Yeah." He said to himself, in a voice that led me to think he didn't believe that to be completely true. He looked out over that deep blue sea, as he spoke to me.

"You know I told you that I was from New York and that's true. That's where I grew up, but I feel like I'm lying a bit when I say it to people. It may be where I'm from, but right here, this ship, this is my home now."

Henry stared out over the ocean. For a minute, he seemed to forget that I was there. I stood for a moment enjoying the silence with him before I interrupted his thoughts.

"It works out well, for you Henry, now you can travel the world and never leave home." I said.

Henry smirked.

"You know, you're right. I am a lucky guy." He said with a smile. "Come on, let me introduce you to some of my friends."

Henry and I meandered back to the front of the ship where the music was playing and the mingling was happening. We approached a wiry, tall guy, with longish hair. He was wearing a tank top, shorts and flip flops. Next to him was a waif of a girl, with short hair and pale skin, in a bikini. Henry introduced me.

"Cal, Milli, this is Martin." Henry said.

Cal quickly sized me up.

"Henry, you old softy. Did you bring home a stray?" he said.

"I met him this afternoon. He's a good guy." Henry defended.

"Oh relax Henry, I'm only kidding. Put er' there Martin." Cal extended his hand. I shook his hand. It was a weak handshake. Cal was all bark.

"Nice to meet you." Cal said.

"Likewise." I added.

"… and this lovely creature is Milli." Henry introduced.

Milli, looked me up and down like a farmer would examine an animal at market. It made me feel a bit uncomfortable, but I didn't show it. She didn't offer her hand she simply said:

"He's cute."

"Easy girl, he just got here." Henry teased.

We left those two and continued to make our way through the crowd. When we were out of earshot Henry whispered to me.

"Cal's family owns one of the largest software companies in Silicon Valley. They had money before, but not like now and Milli's father is a Senator. She'll bang you if she thinks you have money."

"Isn't she rich?" I asked, a bit confused.

"Very." Henry added nonchalantly.

"You and she ever….?" I began to ask. Henry didn't answer, but just gave me a glance and a wink, confirming my suspicions.

Henry pointed out another skinny kid in his twenties, talking to a couple of girls, who were hanging on every word he was saying.

"That's Jackson, he's old oil money and his brother's a minority owner in the New Jersey Nets, can get you kick-ass tickets if you're ever there. That big guy over there, his name is Sam. He's related to the Ford family, played tailback for Michigan."

Henry continued to give me the lowdown on everyone at the party, most of them he'd met in college at Yale. Others were friends of people who he'd met at Yale. It was pretty obvious by the way he introduced me to people that status was very important among this group. It seemed funny to me that the son of a millionaire should feel insecure being around the son of a billionaire. Where I grew up doctors were the rich people and they weren't millionaires. I tried hard not to judge them too much. What would I do if I was born with that much money? Were these people that much different than me? Or was this what I would've become? I didn't dwell on it too much, they seemed open to getting to know me and the truth was, I had never really had friends before and I'd certainly never been to a party like this before. So I just soaked it all in and enjoyed myself. After a while of shaking hands and networking, which is what it felt like it was, Henry and I retired below to the bar and lounge area. The lounge had the most incredibly comfortable leather couches and a big screen TV. The biggest TV I've ever seen actually.

Henry jumped behind the bar and started pulling out the bottles. He looked very comfortable back there.

"So Marty what will you have?" Henry asked.

"How about a gin and tonic Henry."

"One gin and tonic coming right up my friend."

Henry began mixing the drink.

"So what's your dad do?" I asked

"My family owns Zahn Incorporated. We're the biggest toilet manufacturer in North America. My dad runs the company and a bunch of other little ones," Henry confided.

"So as the sons and daughters of the captains of industry, what do you all do?"

Henry smiled.

"You're looking at it my friend."

"So Martin, I've talked too much about my friends and my life, what's your story?" Henry inquired.

"What do you want to know?"

"Well." Henry began. "You say you're from Seattle, how do you like that? "

"It's not bad, but I'm no longer there, so it must not have had everything I needed. "

Henry laughed.

"Yeah, I suppose."

I tried to bring the conversation back to him.

"You're quite a ways from home, you must be looking for something, yeah?"

"Right now, I'm looking for tonic."
"Sorry friend, no gin and tonic today, you like wine?"

"Sure Henry, whatever you got?" I said

"How about a nice cab?" He asked

"Sounds great. "

"So what do you do when you're not on vacation on a Greek island?" Henry asked.

I had put a lot of time into this answer, so it came rather quickly to me.

"I am a venture capitalist." It was vague, but it could explain a lot about my lifestyle.

"Is that right?" Henry answered without looking up from his bottle.

He didn't seem that interested, which was just fine by me. Henry removed the cork expertly and poured me just a bit in my glass. I swirled it, put my nose inside it inhaled deeply and took a sip. I'd seen people drink wine like that in the movies before and I kind of felt like I was in a movie right now, so it seemed appropriate.

"It tastes great. "

I really meant it. I had never been much of a wine guy, but this was the best one I'd ever had. Henry filled the rest of my glass and his. I took another sip.

"Eight hundred bucks a bottle, it better be great." he said.

I nearly spit out that precious libation, then spoke without thinking.

"Wow, that's what I used to make in a month."

Henry looked confused. "Really?" he said.

I briefly considered making up an elaborate story about what I'd just said, but quickly decided the truth would work just as well here.

"Yeah, when I was younger, I worked as a valet."

"A self made man eh? That's very admirable Marty." he raised his glass in a toast.

"To venture capital and the luxury it can afford" Henry toasted.

I smiled but said nothing. I raised my glass took a sip and drank about fifty dollars worth of wine.

It was at this time that the tall kid whom I had met before, Cal, entered the room escorted by two pretty young women.

"Hey love birds, look what we scored." Cal said.

Cal tossed a bag of white powder onto the bar top.

"Excellent!" Henry exclaimed.

Henry opened the bag and took a big whiff of its contents.

"Smells delicious." He said with delight.

"The guy tells me its from Columbia, I have my doubts, but I already tasted it and it's fantastic." Cal said.

Cal emptied the contents of the bag onto the bar top, took a credit card out of his pocket and began to divide the powder into lines. I had never seen cocaine cut into lines before, yet I'd seen enough movies to know instantly that this is what I was looking at. Henry introduced me to the two young ladies. There was a slender blonde girl named Natalia and a busty brunette named Victoria. Both of the girls were stunning. They were Russian and their accents only added to their mystique.

Henry pulled a hundred dollar bill from his wallet, rolled it up and snorted a line.

"What did I tell you, great shit right?" Cal boasted.

"You are not kidding, this stuff is phenomenal!"   Henry agreed.

 "Ladies, please help yourself"

The girls took the offer without a second thought and railed their lines in turn. It appeared I was the only one in the room who was not accustomed to seeing cocaine.

"Where are you ladies from?" I asked.

Victoria answered. I got the feeling that Natalia didn't speak much English.

"We are from Moscow, it is wonderful city, you ever been?" Victoria replied.

"No, but I have always wanted to and if you two are at all representative of the beauty the city has to offer, I won't let another opportunity escape me."

(Was this me talking?)

Victoria smiled at the compliment.

Henry laughed.

"You are very flattering American." Victoria said.

She briefly locked eyes with me, a glance that nearly made my heart stop. Wow, she was sexy. How was it that all of these beautiful people end up in one place? Hmm? If the question I was asking was: "Why are all the people on a 300 foot yacht, anchored on the coast of this vacation resort, beautiful?" I suppose that an easy answer could simply be, " Because they were invited." Henry interrupted my thoughts.
" That is smooth, Marty, you're up champ."
Henry offered the rolled up bill to me. I was instantly frozen with indecision.
"Thanks, but I don't usually." I said.

"Oh come on man, it's not every day we're able to score shit this good." Cal said.

Then Henry started.

"Please, you're insulting me. I'm offering my boat, my wine and my coke...."

"...our Coke." Cal interjected

"Right, "our" coke, only so you can enjoy yourself, you know what they say, "When in Greece.""

I didn't have much experience with drugs at the time, but what I've found is people generally don't like to do drugs alone. It makes them uncomfortable. At this moment I was making everyone around me a bit uncomfortable, or so I thought. I looked up from the line and into the gaze of the stunning Victoria, she smiled at me. That smile should be against the law.

"Is very good." Victoria offered.

"Ah what the hell, why not." I said.

"Ata boy! Go on take that last one. Lets get this party started!"

The world slowed down, no one was paying that much attention to me, but I felt like I was center stage. I watched almost as an independent observer as I lowered the bill to the line, the world kind of went quiet for a brief second, as my mind quickly darted to the opportunity to escape. What were my options, could I still get out of this. I moved closer. I can't believe it. This is actually me. Andy Davis, from Salt Lake City, about to do cocaine! I put that filthy Benjamin up to my nose. I could smell it already, remnants from the last use. I closed my eyes and snorted…..I snapped back to reality, with a choking gasp. I swear that I could *feel* my eyes dilate and *hear* my heart rate jump. I coughed and choked, like the rookie I was.

I rubbed my nose.

"Wow that really burns." I said.

"How do you like that? We popped his cherry!" Cal shouted.

"Is this really your first time?" Henry asked.

"My teeth are starting to go numb." I said.

My heart was racing, but I was starting to feel euphoric already.

Henry laughed.

"Well I guess that answers that. Pretty great huh?"

All I could do was nod my head and feel the strange sensation that was beginning to overwhelm my body. I looked around the room, it seemed a bit brighter now and everyone had gone back to what they were doing, in fact Cal had already began to cut up more lines. I felt a tingling in my extremities and then pressure on my hand. I looked down and noticed that Victoria was holding it.

"Come with me, I show you the rest this place." She said.

I followed Victoria from the room. She took me on a tour of the rest of the boat. I acted like I hadn't already seen it, because I certainly didn't mind being alone with her. I took in the sights and sounds of the party, through the lens of my first serious drug experience, it all seemed very strange and fuzzy, yet so much more fun than it had prior to that line of cocaine shotgunning my brain with dopamine. Victoria was a talker. She told me about how much she liked Greece and how she loved the party and how nice she thought Henry and all of his friends were. I lost track of a lot of what she was saying, as my own altered mind was racing. I even lost track of where she had been leading me, until she stopped abruptly and we were all alone in a corridor.

"...and right here is my room, we need to stop. I have more candy in my room. They probably already finish what we had." she said.

"Ok" was all I was able to get out.

We entered the room that Victoria was staying in, she motioned me over to her bed. "Take seat."

She patted the bed next her.

I sat down and watched as she dug into one of her drawers and pulled out a small vial of coke. She then turned to face me.

"You are very quiet Martin."

"I think people talk too much, you learn more when you listen." I said.

"Is very nice of you to listen to me, but I want you to talk. I love to hear Americans talk. Sound like movie star." She said.

"What would you like me to say?"

"Anything. You think I am pretty? She asked.

"Very." I confided.

"I think you are pretty, Martin."

"Thanks" I said.

Victoria, pulled her shirt over her head, she wore a tight body and a nearly-transparent lacy black bra.

"You think I am sexy?" She asked.

"Very."

"I think you are sexy, Martin."

She sat down onto the bed next to me. I was paralyzed by her confident sexuality. All I could do was watch, and wait and see what she had in store for us. She opened the vial, tapped a bit of the powder onto her finger and snorted it. She closed her eyes and took a deep breath of delight. Then she looked me straight in the eyes, licked her finger and wet a line across her perfect breast, she poured cocaine onto it.

"Would you like another line?" She asked

"Yes" I replied.

It was the only answer I was even remotely capable of giving at that moment. Victoria arched her back and pushed her chest towards the ceiling. I moved towards her and snorted the line off of her breast. She sighed with passion, then looked directly at me one more time.

"You ever been with Russian girl?"

I shook my head, unable to speak as the pleasure of cocaine assaulted my system. She gave me a sultry smile.

"You're about to." She whispered.

Victoria, moved towards me and kissed me. I responded in kind. She moved closer, took my hand and put it on her breast. I had never been the object of so much desire. It was this surreal, euphoric experience, one that I will never forget.

Much of experience is situational and drugs aren't any different. This was my first time doing cocaine, and I spent it having sex all night with the most alluring female I had ever encountered, in her cabin on this incredible yacht...So needless to say I made a positive association with the drug. Now I don't know if you've ever done cocaine, but I will say this about the drug, it is quite the ride. I know what you're thinking, it's addictive. True, but no more addictive than nicotine and we all try that. I recommend doing cocaine one time, you probably won't get into any trouble, but only one time...I did it more than once.

Chapter Eleven
A Playboy's Life Is Easy

I couldn't place that sound. Was someone banging on my door? Why would they do that at this hotel? They never had before. The banging continued, then a voice. "Hey you in there, get up! Breakfast is ready." The voice said.

I grumbled and muttered something to myself about the early maid service, still not fully aware of what was going on. I sat up in bed and looked around. Where was I? This was not my hotel? The events of last night were coming back to me…Victoria, cocaine, sex. Nope, I was not in my hotel, I was on board the Hampton Beauty and I recognized the voice, it came to me.

"Henry?" I said.

He appeared before me.

"Well look what the cat dragged in, I see you had a good night." He said

I looked down and noticed that I was naked but I was covered from the waist down by the blanket and I was alone.

"Good morning Henry." I said.

"Was that a great party or what? " Henry replied.

"I cannot complain one bit, where's Victoria?"

"She and Natalia left this morning to catch their flight. They're going home today." He said.

"Oh really?" I said.

"I hope you're proud of yourself taking advantage of a girl like that." He joked.

"I'm pretty sure that it was the other way around".

"Feeling used are you? " Henry teased.

"Hardly, that was pretty much the best thing that has ever happened to me. Cocaine is a hell of a drug. " I said.

"I can't believe you've never done it. "

"I know, what was I waiting for?" I joked.

Henry laughed at me.

"Marty, you're all right. You know, I don't know what you have planned, but Victoria was using this room and she's gone now. If you want to hang out for a while, you could stay here."

"Oh I don't know Henry, I don't want to get in your way."

"You kidding me? You'd be doing me a favor, I'm bored with everyone around here and you seem to know how to have a good time. I've been trying to bang Victoria for weeks with no luck at all. You must have a chocolate flavored dick or something."

"Just lucky I guess." I replied.

"Well what do you say, you want to stay here? "

"How could I possibly say no, Henry." Henry laughed.

"I wouldn't expect you to. Come on down to breakfast."

And with that Henry left for the galley. While getting dressed, I found the empty vial on the floor next to a pair of Victoria's panties. I smiled to myself, it had been a good night and I had a feeling that being around these people, there were more to come.

It seems to be the case in my life, that things speed up and then they slow down. It is all perception. When you do something new, you soak it all in and pay particular interest to the time. When it's something you do every day, you pay no attention at all. I will never forget my first night on the HAMPTON BEAUTY, but I would spend the better part of the next six months, doing pretty much the same thing.
This was such an interesting group of people. They had traveled the world, seen it all, owned everything that had been invented and moved from one party to the next. None of them had any real responsibilities. Henry liked to think that he was watching after that ship, but really the crew took care of everything. Cal, Milli and Sam and everyone else who filtered on and off of the ship, really did nothing. I mean *nothing* at all. They were doing what I imagine most of us would do given the chance. If

resources and time were not obstacles, we would fall into this life of leisure and hedonism. The drugs would follow, as they are a cure for the boredom that comes with the package.

We would spend our nights partying on board and occasionally we would mix it up by partying at one of the bars on the island. We would sleep until noon, spend the day drinking coffee and shaking off hangovers. If the nights were particularly light, we might find time to do some snorkeling, or buzz around on a jet ski.

Henry took me scuba diving a few times. That was a unique experience, a lot like being on another planet. So to say we did nothing, I guess would be a bit of a misnomer. We just did nothing of value to anyone. We did not work. Everything was for our own benefit. It was all to easy too fall into a life where you only cared about your-self and your personal gratification. Yes, over the next months, I lived a life I thought I had always wanted. All I did was play. Henry and I got really close. I could tell he was looking for a friend. For some reason he felt like I wasn't just using him for his toys, even though I stayed on that ship night in and night out without paying rent just like everyone else. I listened to him. I think that was important to him. No one else of the "do nothing crew" ever did. We had a great time together. Funny that coming from such different backgrounds, we had so much in common. He was a hedonistic playboy, but he also had a philosophical side. He and I spent many nights top deck under the stars, discussing what life was "all about" sometimes until the sun came up. Cocaine will make you talk all night. I grew good at talking a lot, but not about myself.

Henry was a drug addict. Most of us were, though I don't think any of us recognized it. We did some kind of drug every day. Even if it was only alcohol, but it was rarely ever just alcohol. I too was becoming an addict. I didn't think that I needed the drugs, but I also never said no to them. I just had a better time on them than off. It also began to feel completely normal now that everyone around me was on them all the time as well. These were my days, this was my life. It was a great time. I cared for nothing outside of our little bubble. I thought no further ahead than the evening.

One rainy morning, Henry came to me and told me that we were pulling anchor. He said that Santorini was getting stale and that it was time to move on to greener pastures. We were going to Spain, specifically a place called "Ibiza." I didn't know at the time, but something was waiting for us in Ibiza. It had brought leaders to their knees, destroyed hearts, empires and Beatles. It was the most powerful force in man's simple little world. A woman.

Chapter Twelve
A Rose By Any Other Name...

We had traveled a long way to get here. Living on the boat full-time, I had come to consider myself quite the sailor. I was kidding myself. I was simply a passenger and it was proved to me when we had some pretty rough seas off the coast of Sicily which made us so sick that for an entire day I saw only the inside of my room and the bottom of my toilet. It didn't affect the crew; apparently seasickness is something you get used to. We sailed to places in the Mediterranean where we could see no land at all, there was something intriguing about being out of sight of shore. It's a strange feeling to see nothing but blue in three hundred and sixty degrees. Sometimes I would climb up to the front of the ship, lean over the bow and watch the water running past below. It would come rushing towards me and then retreat once again, as our ship buoyed up and down on the ocean swells. I love the smell of the salty mist that sprays up from the ship, cutting through those powerful waves.

    The voyage took about a week and when we arrived in Ibiza, it was exactly what I had expected. It had beautiful beaches with crystal clear blue water, sunny weather and a lot of young drunk Europeans with a few Americans mixed in. I'm not complaining, but it did seem a lot like Santorini, only with Spaniards running the show. Everyone on board knew what we were doing here. This is where Rose was spending her summer away from graduate school.

Rose was the perfect name for her, she stood out among the flowers of this little garden. She was as florid and elegant, with a scent just as sweet. Everyone in the "do nothing club" loved her. She was witty and charming, sexy without trying and had a luminous smile that brightened the life of all those fortunate to be within sight. She was everything that a man was supposed to want in a woman. While everyone said they loved Rose, the only one who honestly meant it was Henry. He adored her, Shakespeare would have described her as his moon, his sun, but to Henry she was his un-railed line of cocaine, her allure seductive, her effect intoxicating and his addiction undeniable.

Most women were attracted to Henry, he was young, good looking and powerful. He could offer any woman he met, witty banter, political philosophy, jewelry, art, a wardrobe from Milan and a life-time of leisure. His studies of philosophy undoubtedly lead him to the capitalist braying of Adam Smith and the theory of supply and demand. Rose had all of these things that Henry possessed. She didn't desire typical material pursuits, she had them in abundance, in fact, Henry had nothing that she desired. It is unlikely that Rose herself could have vocalized the thing that she wanted, like a dream that was powerful yet difficult to recall. Something got Rose up in the morning, something was out there that she couldn't put her finger on yet made her incomplete and Henry didn't have it. I did.

I avoided her like the plague, I was indifferent to her stories that captivated everyone else. I often found her loud and self-centered, I resented her popularity and the ease at which confidence and happiness had come in her life. I went about my business (that is the business of nothing) as if she were not on the ship. My mornings were spent sleeping off hangovers, my afternoons were spent reading or playing games, Henry loved to play chess and hit me up for a game as often as I was willing. My nights were spent in the self-destructive decadence that few ever fully know, like that of a rockstar or movie god. It was sex and drugs and…you know the rest.

    In spite of my efforts, it seemed every time I turned around Rose was there. To her I was an enigma, as I was to many of the "do nothing club". I was vague about my background and family and job, as a full time liar it is best to only give information about your past when really prodded. Lucky for me, the majority of people were usually more than willing to allow the conversation to become about them. I've found that "themselves" is the favorite topic of conversation for almost everyone. If you keep asking questions, they will keep answering. I was able to learn a lot about people this way and it made them like me, even though I didn't have much to say. Rose loved to talk about herself and so she loved to talk to me. Rose would open up to me in ways I doubt she opened up to anyone. I listened because I was polite, not but because I really cared. She seemed sheltered and naïve, but she was so charming and beautiful. She was a petite woman, with chin length auburn hair, emerald eyes, silky smooth skin and the face of an angel. I almost resented her for being so pretty. It's like she had this power over me. I found her stories banal, yet I couldn't help but be physically attracted to her. I also knew that

Henry would be crushed if I ever acted on my desires.

Perhaps I lead her on more than I was willing to admit. I was very nice to her. I laughed at her jokes, offered her advice when she asked my opinion. I was even a shoulder for her to cry on when she told me about her brother.

Rose's brother had been killed because the people of our country had traded the immorality of getting blow jobs in the White House for the immorality of dropping bombs on innocent brown people who look a lot like brown people from a different place that they were mad at. Sometimes in the process of bombing the brown people who looked like the other brown people that they are mad at, they accidentally bomb their own. Her brother was one of those accidents. He was her only sibling and apparently they had been really close.

Maybe my animosity toward her ran deeper than I thought, maybe she was a reflection. Was I as selfish as her? What had she done that was selfish? She talked a lot about herself, but was it so bad? I on the other hand had disappeared into the night and left my entire life behind me and never told a soul. I tried not to think about it much, but what were my parents thinking right now? JD? They probably assume I'm dead, in many ways, that man they knew was dead. But was that fair? Thinking about it made me feel awful and so the more time I spent with Rose, the worse I felt. My days began to become hard. The life of leisure and hedonism was losing its luster. The banality of the conversation was becoming so obvious I couldn't ignore it. It was all, "Man, I was so high last night." or "You know, for a five-star restaurant, it really wasn't that great." "There's no good shopping anywhere on the island."

Our connections were shallow, our complaints trite and deep down all of us knew it.

    I tried desperately to escape the growing anxiety I felt. To fill the void I started doing even more drugs, ecstasy one night, cocaine the next and alcohol in between. I was going downhill and the depression was coming back. I began feeling just as worthless as I did when I was a valet. Was I any different, masquerading as bourgeois?

    Henry's love of attrition was wearing him down and every attempt he made to bring Rose closer only pushed her further away. She was a puzzle he couldn't solve, the one item in this world he couldn't buy. His obsession with what he couldn't have began to inundate him. One night it all blew up. He finally came clean, he told Rose the way he really felt and she told him the way she really felt. She loved him like a brother, but they were never going to be more than that. The news sent him straight to a bottle and Rose straight to me.

    Rose was in tears when she knocked on my door. Upon learning that he could never have her, Henry had said some mean things. She was upset and confused. She trusted me, I comforted her. I gave her a big hug and let her cry. When she had said all she had come to say, she pulled away from me. Looked at me with those beautiful eyes and told me she loved me. I never said it back, but again, I misled her. I couldn't resist her any longer. I gave her what she wanted. Maybe it was what I wanted too. I kissed her softly at first and then passionately. That night she made love to me and I had sex with her. When it was over, I got dressed and left her asleep in my bed, I took a walk topside to clear my head.

    It was late, bordering on early and everyone had gone to sleep. A full moon gave texture to the water and the sound of the ocean was all I could hear, it was incredibly peaceful. I found Henry passed out in a deck chair cradling a bottle of wine. As I approached him, he awoke.

"Martin? That you?" He squinted to see me in the moonlight.

"Hey Henry. How are you doing?" I asked.

"Oh I've been better, friend. You want some wine?"

"Sure." I said.

I took the bottle from him and had a swig. Henry took the bottle back and took a long drink, he was very drunk already. I had a moment of fraternal concern.

"Maybe you should take it easy on that stuff, bud." I said.

"Maybe next life my brother, maybe next life…life, life…It's all easy, my life, easy. You know what I do Marty? "

"No Henry. "

"Nothin, I don't do *anything*...This is it...You're new, but this is it. My dad keeps a huuuuge stash of cash in a house aaand every few months, I stop in and I borrow some and every time I go back it's replenished, like a money tree. I never even have to see him. I never have to ask him for anything. I haven't even spoken to him in three, no five months."

Henry took another long drink of wine and then slumped back and closed his eyes.

"Yup, as long as I don't bother him or embarrass him the money keeps coming...There's over ten million dollars there. You know how much that is Marty?"

"No." I answered honestly.

It's a lot! ...or nothing... I don't know...he loves me though, he does...

"I'm sure he does Henry."

"He doesn't say it, but he does...I know it...it's the code, my birthday...code to the money tree."

I absorbed everything he said that night, though the ramifications of it all wouldn't become clear to me until later.

"Let's get you to bed huh?" I offered.

"Good idea, Marty...good..."

He trailed off. I lifted him over my shoulder and helped walk him to bed. When I put him down, he awoke again, for just a moment.

"Marty...Marty wait..." He mumbled.

"Yes, Henry?"

"You're my best friend..." Henry said.

He then curled up and went to sleep. Those words cut me like a knife. What had I done?! I had slept with the only girl he had ever loved. I didn't love her. Why did I do it? Was it purely animalistic? Did I simply give in to the natural order? A sexy female, a red blooded man? I wish it were that simple. If I were to be honest, I think I did it because I was jealous of Henry. He had everything and I had nothing. I wanted the one thing he couldn't have. I used Rose to do it. Poor Rose, she didn't deserve it. She was a nice girl. I used her! I was the selfish one! I was the one I hated! My mind raced, my heart pounded, I felt short of breath as if I had the weight of the world resting on m chest. I began physically shaking as I walked away from Henry's room. Soon I was in tears. I needed to do... something, right now. I needed to leave this place!... and so I did.

    Just as before, I disappeared. I walked off that ship and never returned, leaving my best friend, two broken hearts and a piece of my soul behind.

Chapter Thirteen

Synchronicity

For the first time in five years, I found my feet firmly planted on the grand old soil of the United States. I had been gone for over five years, but this place still felt like home. I was in New York City, which is as close to a foreign country as you can get and still be in America. I had never been to New York before, but it still felt comfortable. It was nice to hear people speaking English, I didn't have to struggle to understand or communicate. The familiarity of the culture was nice, but coming here did little to make me feel any better. I checked into the Waldorf, intent on wasting the last of my money in a blaze of glory. I dressed in my finest suits and spent my nights hitting the hot clubs in town to drink and drink and score some blow. I bought my very first prostitute. She wasn't a corner crack ho, she was the gorgeous high class, good enough for a governor type. She cost me two grand. It was fun for the moment, but no drug or woman could keep me from thinking about how it all ended that night on board the Hampton Beauty. I felt empty. I was a shell. I smiled when I had to, was polite to those I was systematically giving the rest of my money to. I didn't care if I lived or died, I finished the rest of my coke and checked out of my hotel room. Just down the street from the hotel I found a local liquor store and spent my last twenty bucks on a cheap bottle of whiskey, as a matter of fact it was Old Granddad's whiskey, the stuff I'd been drunk on the very first time when I was 17. That was 13 years ago, what had I done since then? What have I accomplished? No one would miss me if I was gone. My parents may have at one time, but I am sure they assumed I was dead long ago. I unscrewed the cap to the bottle and took a slam off of it. Even as bad as I felt, the cocaine and whiskey helped to numb me. I looked around at the swarms of people on the street, everyone had somewhere to go, but not me. So with no direction, I started walking, I walked myself to Central Park, past the Imagine monument; John Lennon, there was a man who'd done something with his time on this earth. The complete antithesis to me, there were flowers and candles next to it and several people gathered around... What did he have ?

He inspired people. Why was a man like that so easy for others to love?

I saw a crazy man fishing in Jackie Onassis Lake, well at least I assumed he was crazy, were there any fish in this lake?

I walked and I walked fast. Everyone here walks fast. A cop looked at me once as I staggered and sipped my bottle. I could see him consider asking me about the bag and being drunk in public, but it probably seemed that a man in a two thousand dollar suit was more trouble than it's worth. Maybe a lawyer, someone with means or someone not to be messed with. He said nothing and continued on his way.

I was completely inebriated, my mind was spinning. I looked at the bottle, it was only about a quarter gone. A thought occurred to me. At this rate, the bottom of this bottle could mean the end. This made me smirk, I took another long swig and felt it burn down my throat.

    The night wore on and the people I passed became fewer and fewer. I didn't notice that the buildings around me were now deteriorating, the people began to look less and less friendly. I was oblivious, I didn't notice anyone around me, but for once, someone noticed me.

    It hadn't occurred to me that I was now the only white guy on the street and I was certainly the only one wearing an Armani suit. Downtown I was just another face. What I didn't know was that I was in Harlem now and in Harlem, I was a target. In fact, I had already been marked by a guy passing me on a street corner a few blocks down. He had noticed me and subtly made a text message and now I was being followed. My legs were wobbly and vision blurry. The cocaine had worn off and my mind wasn't sharp, I wandered off of the main street and into an alley to relieve myself behind a dumpster. I checked the level in my whiskey bottle, my eyes refused to focus, there was still quite a bit left, enough to do the job and end my misery, but before I had a chance to house that final drink, I heard a voice from behind me that saved my life... for the moment.

"Hey, you got a light man?" the voice said.

I turned to see a man in front of me holding a cigarette. I didn't have a lighter, but instinctively looked down and patted my pockets, but that's actually what the man wanted. He was a distraction, I felt the blow from the back of my head, pain radiated through my skull, I dropped immediately to the ground, the assault didn't stop there. I felt the blows rain down on me, punches and kicks, I was grateful for the half bottle of whiskey in my blood. It was making the worst beating of my life very bearable. I heard shouts from the darkness, but saw nothing. I was in the fetal position, protecting my face.

"Fuck him up!"

"Get his wallet!"

The faceless voices yelled from the dark.

There were multiple voices, I couldn't tell how many, but I knew I was being hit by more than one person. The beating stopped, I was hit in the face with something soft, it was my wallet.

"Where's your money white boy!!" Another voice shouted angrily.

The wallet, it was empty. I had forgotten. All this trouble and these thieves would get nothing. I didn't respond, I couldn't move, I couldn't feel much, but what little I could feel was pain. I lay on the ground and awaited my fate.

I heard the action of a gun. A bullet being chambered.

"He ain't got shit Q"! A voice called out. I recognized it as the one who'd asked for a light.

"Should we do him?"

I was all ears for the answer to this question, I was in pain, miserable, but not scared. I had intended this to be my last night on earth, so while it wasn't going to plan, I may still get my wish.

Silence.

Why was no one responding? My death was being considered. A cost benefit analysis on my demise was happening right before me. Who were these people? I thought for sure this would be an easy decision, after all, what value did my life have to my assailants?

"Hey, what's going on back here?" A new voice, I thought, one that seemed oddly familiar.

"Mind your own business!" This one came from the one called Q.

"I can't mind my own business, this is my neighborhood and I'm involved now." The man said.

I knew that voice, where did I know that voice, it was so dark back here, I opened my eyes, a gun was pointed at my head, there were four or five other men standing around me. One at least who didn't want me dead.

"This has got nothin to do with you brother, so just keep walking," Q said.

"You got his wallet, now let him go," my friend said.

I managed to look up, my face was covered in blood, but I could see now that guns were pointed at my new friend.

"You really want to get involved? What's one less white boy mean to you?" Q said.

"It doesn't mean anything, but one less murder on my block means a lot." The man offered.

"Does it mean fifty bucks?"

"If that's what it takes."

And that is how my life was bought for fifty bucks, that was less money than I'd spent on cocaine that very night. Q and the other assailants left, because they were paid by a stranger. This stranger, with the warm voice, who was now helping me to my feet pulled me out of the alley and leaned me up against a street light. I turned and vomited right there on the side walk, filling your stomach full of whiskey and then getting kicked in it repeatedly will do that to a man.

My savior, the one with that soothing voice spoke.

"Ah man, you look like shit, what the hell are you doing out here?"

I took my sleeve and wiped my mouth and did my best to clear the blood from my eyes. I looked up at this man for the first time.

"I think you're going to be all right, but I'll take you to a hospital if you.... whoa, no way! No way! Andy? Impossible! Andy, is that you?"

The massive man towering over me had a face I knew all too well.

"JD?" I muttered weakly.

Then darkness overwhelmed me.

Chapter Fourteen

Second Life...Or Third?

I opened my eyes with difficulty, squinting to keep the pain of light to a minimum. There was a scent of something in the air and the faint sound of water boiling. I never knew that a human being could feel as awful as I did just then. The pain in my head was only being lessened by the distraction of pain all over my body, I felt nauseous, as if I could vomit at any moment, I tasted the acrid bile in my mouth. Apparently I already had been. With extreme effort I opened my eyes up wide enough to take in my surroundings. I was lying on an old sofa, there was a bucket on the floor next to me. I was in a small apartment. Everything looked old and used, but clean and neat at the same time. The decor could have passed for something that would have been hip in the seventies. It reminded me of my grandmothers house. She had red carpet like this place, and an orange couch with a flower pattern on it and wallpaper...this place had wall paper, you don't see that everyday. I could see a small window with a fire escape and the lights of the city shining through. It was still night time, but what day was it? The nausea overwhelmed me again, I instinctively grabbed the bucket next to me and dry heaved for a minute, nothing came out, I was all out of stomach contents it appeared. I looked up from the bucket to meet the eyes of a little girl. She had pigtails, wore a nightgown decorated with unicorns and stars.

She hugged a teddy bear close to her side and had a binky in her mouth. She pointed at me and said something unintelligible. The noise caught the attention of someone in the next room. A tall woman entered the room from the kitchen, She was older, late sixties I would guess. She had a pretty face, but one that looked tired. It also looked warm and friendly, even though she shook her head when she looked at me with what I guess you could call caring, motherly disgust.

Then she turned her attention to the girl. The little girl pointed at me and repeated her binky mumble.

"Mmmm..." The little girl said.

The woman spoke to her.

"Where did you get that? I thought we talked about this? We know that big girls don't use binkies, right?"

The little girl nodded.

"Give it to me."

She reluctantly gave the woman her binky.

"Now, what were you trying to say?"

She pointed at me again.

"Ewww!!"

The woman laughed.

"Eww, is right honey, the fool is awake." She said.

The little girl coughed violently for a moment.

"Did you take your medicine this morning?" The woman demanded.

The little girl shook her head.

"And why not?"

"It tastes gwoss"

"My nana gave that to me when I was your age. It will help with that cough, go on now. Don't make me ask twice."

The girl relented and left the room. Presumably to take her medicine. The woman turned her attention back to me, she offered me a cup of something that I hadn't even noticed she was carrying.

"Here, drink this."

I sat up and took the cup from her.

"Thank you."

"It talks, too" she said.

It was soup, chicken noodle, from the smell. I took a sip. It tasted amazing and it was something that my stomach was willing to accept. Of course it would have probably been ok with any non-alcoholic substance by this point.

"So boy, just a piece of advice. Next time you decide to make a damn fool of yourself with that booze, you might want to make sure you don't get lost. A boy like you can get killed walking out there at night, this ain't Soho."

I nodded my head and took another sip. The events of the night before came back to me, but with spotty recollection.

"My name is Martin, thank you for the soup."

"Martin? Jonathan said your name was Andy. The way you looked when he brought you in here, he may have mistaken you for Gandhi. Whatever your name is, you're welcome."

The little girl returned from the next room with a sour face.

"Did you drink it all?"

The girl nodded.

"That's a good girl."

I interrupted.

"Did you say Jonathan?"

"Yes, Jonathan, my nephew. He went out to fetch you some medicine, should be back anytime. My name is Mary and this here is Janie."

Janie, who was already sucking her thumb, smiled and waved at me with her free hand. She was about the most adorable little girl I'd ever seen. I hadn't dreamt it, it was real. The memory of JD helping me last night. How on earth did I end up here?

JD returned with some antiseptic and bandages, the cuts on my hands and face were numerous, but not deep. The alcohol stung the scrapes on my cheek. JD recounted for me what he'd been up to. It seemed as though he'd moved back home to help his Aunt, who was raising his niece Janie. She was getting on in years and was having trouble keeping up with her, as she was only three now. Janie's mother Robin had died in a car accident two years ago. Janie had some kind of respiratory condition that kept her from feeling well most of the time and it ended up being a full time job to look after her. Mary was a retired schoolteacher and now she was taking care of Janie. JD had moved in after the accident to help her and had quickly taken to his niece and treated her like his own. He had been working at a garage fixing cars until he was laid off a few months back. Now they were just doing their best to get by and save some money so that little Janie could go see a specialist about her illness. Most days though it seemed they were never going to be able to afford it. Janie had been in and out of the hospital her whole life and the cost was crippling. These two were doing what they could and everyone kept good spirits but his aunt looked older than her years.

    JD brought me up to speed on what was going on back home. He failed to mention my parents, I suppose he would've spoken of them if I had asked. The truth was I really didn't want to know, the thought of it was too painful for me. He was less interested in telling me about his life than he was hearing about mine. He told me they thought I had died that night at the restaurant. Some people thought I was involved, but everyone just assumed I was either dead or on the run and most people thought I was dead.

"Where have you been?" He finally said bluntly.

I thought long and hard about this answer before I spoke. Finally, I took a deep breath and began...

I gave him the Cliff's Notes of the last five years of my life but really didn't say anything. How could you possibly describe it? I had assumed a completely different identity, lived a completely different life. I always remember being paralyzed when I hadn't seen someone for two weeks and they asked me what I was up to. What is anyone up to? How do you describe it? You get up, have breakfast, go to a job, come home, watch tv, hit the repeat button. That hadn't exactly been my life, but when I was on the ship it was something similar, just far more hedonistic. I didn't speak of Rose, it was too soon. JD watched my gaze drift, indicating that my mind had gone to that place it goes, that darker place. He brought me back with a joke, that brought a smile and a laugh. He was a good friend, I had betrayed him too. I had left him alone, with no explanation and after five years he wasn't even asking for one now. I guess he just figured that if I wanted to explain myself I would. He was very wise, I knew he was good with people, he always had been. Only now was I starting to understand why. He let people be what they wanted and do what they wanted, he let people be free, free of judgement about their lifestyles and their choices. It takes a wise person to understand that the choices others have made in their lives are theirs alone and are not for all.

This subtle understanding and acceptance of the differences and imperfections in us all was what drew others to him like a magnet.

He was talking again, but I had stopped listening, I was thinking that what he had was rare and there was this unclear thought in the back of my head I couldn't quite turn into words...but he could use it for more than just fixing cars, I could use it for something... the thought was gone, I was interrupted by JD's aunt, firmly letting us know that it was late and that I should get some rest. I couldn't argue, I was running on alcohol and adrenaline only and it was just about to wear off. So we said good night. As I slept on the couch, in that dingy Harlem apartment, my mind wandered, I had strange dreams, dreams of better days in the past and the future. My subconscious knew before I did that I had been given a second chance at life and this time I needed to do something with it. The details were not clear yet, but something big was about to happen, I could feel it.

I spent the next week convalescing and catching up with my old friend. He didn't prod me any more about what I had been doing or why I had left everyone behind. JD had this gift, he never asked for anything more than to share your time. He spoke of the problems his aunt and niece were having, they had medical problems. His aunt was retired, but still worked part time at a local deli in order to keep the family afloat. The way he explained it, it wasn't a complaint, he was simply laying out the facts and only because I would ask him about it. It was hard times in Harlem and his family was feeling it just like everyone else.

After hearing about the serious financial problems of his family and basically everyone in the city, it seemed amazing to me that I had squandered a small fortune in just a few years. I really had none of it left, so for the past week I had been one more burden for JD and his aunt, but not for long.

I hadn't been sleeping much since I arrived in this quaint apartment. At night my mind was scattered and restless, I felt anxious. I know that it was in part because I was going through withdrawals. It wasn't just my abrupt sobriety though, it was more than that. I saw JD and his family and this town and this world as just a puzzle to be solved. There was a way to make things better for these people, I was sure of it. How? What could I do for them?

You can volunteer in a community for a lifetime and it wouldn't do a fraction of what a philanthropist could do with a signature on a piece of paper or the cutting of a ribbon...That was it! I needed money, *a lot* of it, it was so simple. I sat right up in bed, this was a perfect plan. I ran to JD's room and burst through the door!

"JD" I said in a shouted whisper.

JD stirred in his bed and grumbled.

"Yeah man, what is it?"

"I have the answer to all of our problems, get up!"

"Seriously?" He asked, still half-asleep.

"Yes!"

Chapter Fifteen

No Going Back

With a little more coaxing I was able to get the sleeping giant from his bed. I made some coffee and kept him up all night explaining the plan. In the beginning, he laughed at my ideas. It soon became clear however that I was dead serious. I spoke with quite the cavalier tone of things that to the average listener would have been morally suspect at best and could land both of us in a federal penitentiary or grave at worst. In the end he let me finish my rant and it went something like this:

"The rent, the medical bills, the drug dealers, car thieves, murderers, thugs of all varieties of ills can be solved by one simple solution, money! I can't get enough to fix everything, but I know where we can get a lot, more than you've ever seen and the owner would never miss it! Well he would miss it, but he doesn't need it, not by a long shot."

    I explained that the money I was speaking of just sat in a house and only represented a small fraction of what this guy was worth. Best of all I knew the code, we could rob this guy without having to break into anything. It was perfect. I of course was speaking of Henry's father.

JD was not keen on the idea in the beginning.

"This is wrong." He said simply.

"Why?" I asked.

JD shook his head and sighed.

"What has happened to you Andy? That you even ask? It's wrong because it's not *our* money."

I rolled my eyes.

"Please, you should see how these people waste it, $5,000 dollar call girls, mansions in ten different countries, yachts the size of Manhattan. It may be his money, but he doesn't *need* it. We do."

I was getting to him, but wasn't quite there. It was time to pull at the heart strings.

"This money could really help Janie."

JD took a pause.

I had him.

It may have been his love of family that convinced him in the end, but the truth is he'd known me long enough to know that, the way I was talking, I was going to do it anyway.

"All right, someone's got to make sure you don't get killed. When?" He asked.

"I can find the house, no need to case it. There is a security guard at the front gate. No one even lives there most of the year. We can hike in from the backyard, we don't need to break in or anything, I have the security code."

"How much do you think? fifty, a hundred thousand?" JD asked.

"No, *a lot* of money?" I said.

"Fifty thousand dollars isn't a lot of money to you?" He responded dryly.

I thought about the money I had blown

through in the last year and smiled.

"Not any more."

As confident as I felt about being able to pull it off, the night of my first burglary was very exciting. JD and I were silent as we drove to the house. We were both dressed in black, we looked cool, like secret agents... or thieves. We parked the car on the side of the road, a few miles from the gate. The plan was to cut through the woods that surrounded the house and enter the yard through the back. The hike through the brush took longer than I thought. Our headlamps didn't reveal every branch or rock in our path and both of us took a few scrapes and scratches before we got to the wall.

JD scaled the wall with ease and then helped me over. I approached the back door with trepidation and felt a moment of panic as floodlights exposed us. I caught my breath. Just sensor lights. JD looked just like I felt, the lights had scared him too. I approached the key pad next to the door I took a deep breath, exhaled and punched in the code, it took just a moment to process before the screen read: "Welcome Henry." The door opened into the downstairs kitchen. We stopped and listened.

It was silent, not a sound. I still felt the need to be cautious, this house was so big that someone could be home and I'd never know it. JD and I entered the great room on the basement floor.

The place was spartan, with an enormous chandelier in the middle of the room. Suits of armor stood in the corners of the room. Suits of armor for crying out loud! It's like we were breaking into the home of Citizen Kane. We made our way through this creepy house that looked like it belonged more to a lord from the middle ages rather than a toilet manufacturing magnate. We arrived at the master bedroom.

All was just as it was described by Henry my

last night on board the Hampton Beauty. There was another key pad behind a painting on the south wall. One last obstacle. I punched in Henry's birthday again. the hidden wall cracked open. My heart was beating now. I looked at JD and smiled. We entered the room. It was small, but full of various items that looked expensive, watches and jewelry, some sculptures, a signed copy of "A Hard Days Night" on vinyl. In the back of the room, sitting on a desk was an ordinary looking briefcase. I didn't come here for stuff to fence, I came here for cash and a vague plan on what I would do with it. The briefcase wasn't locked. I popped the latch, my heart was pounding, I felt like Indiana Jones uncovering lost treasure in some ancient tomb. I half expected a giant boulder to come rolling down the hall. I opened it slowly. The light was low in this little vault, but my eyes quickly met what they were looking for, cash...a whole lot of cash.

Chapter Sixteen

Between PR

"No." JD said firmly.

He sat opposite me at a table in this busy little coffee and bagel place down the street from his apartment. He looked like he meant it, this was going to take some convincing. I was becoming accustomed to getting my way, but this was definitely going to take some work.

A friend of mine told me once, that "A loner is just a leader, who doesn't want followers." I didn't want followers, in fact I kind of resented followers. I didn't care if people paid attention to me, but I wanted to be heard. I couldn't influence people like the JD's of the world. He was charismatic and people wanted to please him. They naturally believed that he was someone who new "the way", someone who should be followed. I was a leader, but not the right kind. If I was going to make a difference, if I was going to shape the world in the image of my choosing, I was going to need him. I couldn't help the people of this neighborhood, my heart was in the right place, but my skin was the wrong color. They would never accept it, they wouldn't trust me and if I were going to accomplish the schemes my mind was currently conjuring, I needed the trust of the people. JD was the perfect candidate. He was from this neighborhood. He was somewhat of a local legend at his old high school for leading his football team to state.

They knew his family, his aunt was well known and liked. She had lived on this same block her whole life. She was sixty-three years old now, that is enough time to even get to know a good portion of the people in a city the size of Harlem. She would be an asset as well, but there was something else I needed and it started with JD. I needed to find Q.

"That is a bad idea." He continued.
"You are out of your element Andy, this is the man who would have killed you like he was swatting a fly."
"That is exactly why we need him." I replied.

I had asked a lot of my friend. I understood this. At this exact moment in time, there was millions in stolen money sitting under his bed. It was enough to make me a little nervous too. I needed a meeting with Q, just a meeting and I knew that JD could find him. I continued to state my case.

"I know that this sounds crazy, but stupid people act on their emotions all day long, smart people are those who can control them and make sound, rational choices. This guy is a business man. He will listen to me."

"Or kill you." he added.

For a man who not long ago was ready to give up on life, this last comment meant something to me. I didn't want to die now, I had things to do and somehow felt like I knew what I was doing.

"Or kill me... But where's the money in that?" I asked.

JD let out a deep sigh, looked me dead in the eye and nodded.

Later that same night I found myself in front of a building that I thought had to be abandoned, maybe it was. Two tough looking guys held the wall up next to the entrance, casually smoking cigarettes and laughing about something. Above their heads I noticed a security camera, it looked new and out of place. This had to be it. I took a step forward, my movement was abruptly stopped by a hand on my chest. JD, I had forgotten that he was even there.

"When we get in there, you let me do the talking at first." he said.

I nodded.

" I mean it Andy."

I nodded again, but was barely listening, I had laser-like focus when I got a plan stuck in my head. Right now the laser was pointed at that front door.

    We approached the door. The two men looked up, they were guards or dealers, maybe both. JD spoke.
    "Hey man, I need to see Q."
    "Never heard of him." One of the men lied.
    "Maybe I can help you, whatchu looking fo?"
    JD presented a hundred dollar bill. He pulled it taught from its two ends.
    "I'm looking for Q. Tell him John from 133rd street wants to see him."

    The guard looked me up and down. I could read his thoughts: ..."a white guy in this neighborhood, this time of night, didn't look like I wanted to buy product. A cop? "

He shared a glance with his friend, took the money and disappeared around the side of the building.

It was awkward waiting for the man to return. The second dealer who had never given his name, stood there smoked his cigarette and just stared at us, I tried to pretend I didn't notice. I looked around, feigning interest in my surroundings. A homeless guy pushed a cart full of his possessions across the street. Somewhere in the distance I could here what sounded like two cats fighting. It couldn't have been more than a minute or two, but it felt like an hour.

The man returned.

"Arms up." he said flatly.

JD raised his arms and nodded for me to do the same. I complied and the man gave us both a pat down.

"Follow me." He barked once he had finished.

He lead us up the stairs of this old building, while his buddy walked behind us. The place was a dive and the inside was no nicer than the outside. It was dusty and the floorboards creaked as we passed over them. We approached a door that looked out of place. It looked new and solid, reinforced, bulletproof maybe. Our guide knocked on the door.

Another man opened it and let us in. The inside of this room definitely did not fit the décor of the building, everything was clean and new. It had the feel of more of a Park Avenue penthouse. The room was spacious, there was a pool table in the back, a wet bar, leather couches and a big screen TV. A few guys shooting pool stopped and stared as we entered. A well dressed man sat on the couch. This place had the feel of a typical deluxe apartment, aside from the sawed off shotgun conspicuously present on the coffee table. The man in front of the gun stood up as we entered, this was the man we'd come to see.

"Little Johnnie football star! Didn't think I'd be running into you again so soon. To what do I owe the pleasure?"

"I am here Q... *we* are here, because we have a business proposition for you."

"Business? I know your boy, we ain't never met formally, but I know him and last we met we gave him the business. In my experience I see a man at my door after that, it's cuz he lookin to even the score."

Q looked me right in the eyes.

"You lookin to get even?"

I shook my head.

The room was silent while Q took his time evaluating me and his next move. I wasn't scared, in fact I suddenly felt myself getting angry. This neighborhood was covered with filth and his hands weren't clean. He may not have caused the plight of this city, but he was doing his part. He'd jacked me and was willing to kill me just because I got lost in his part of town, I could have been anybody!

Q began again.

"Let me tell you a story...."

My emotion overcame me. I interrupted.

"...Is this a sob story? Because I hate sob stories about crack dealers." (Wow! Did I just say that?!)

Q's crew reached for their guns, JD closed his eyes and shook his head, anticipating his friend being turned into a human bullet sponge. This was surreal, but I had the high of adrenaline coursing through my veins and I was not afraid. If I was going to leave this world I wasn't going to do it cowering. I stared right at him, my face stoic, my breath even. I awaited his response.

To the surprise of us all, Q just laughed.

"Hah, you hate sob stories about crack dealers, do you?"

The tension in the room eased some.

I shrugged my shoulders.

"That and romantic comedies."

"JD, I like this cracker, he's either got a death wish or a set on him like a bull. I'll listen to your proposition."

I could hear JD breathe a sigh of relief and I also noticed some of the guns that had been drawn were now finding their way back to their hiding places. I cleared my throat and began like this:

" Mr. Q."

Q laughed again and shook his head.

"It's just Q man, ain't no misters or sirs round here, feel me?"

"Yes, I feel you, no problem."

Everyone knew that Q had gotten the name "Q" because he had been hustled once at pool and had rewarded the clever guy by beating him to death with a pool cue. Everyone knew this because Q told them and it was an easy enough story to believe about one of the most feared men in Harlem. This however never actually happened. It turns out that he was a huge Trekkie, regularly attended conventions and always wanted to be like this omnipotent alien named "Q" from Star Trek: The Next Generation. I would find this out in later talks, when we discovered that we had more in common than was immediately obvious.

" I feel you Q."

The words were his and felt foreign in my mouth. I needed to relax and speak my own way. I had a plan and it was a good one. I continued.

"...So, I look around this neighborhood and I see run down buildings, crumbling sidewalks, garbage stacked six feet high..."

I glanced around the room at the company I was keeping.

"...and dangerous-looking men on every corner."

"You got a point white-boy, or you just come down here to talk noise 'bout my town?" Q snapped.

"Yeah, I have a point. It doesn't have to be like this. It can be better...I know that you sell crack, at least...anyway. I want to employ you."

Q did not answer. For a moment he just stared at me like I was an alien. In his little world he was king and used to knowing how to deal with most anything that happened in his kingdom. Rival dealers, junkies, cops, these were what he understood. He did not know what to make of me. After what felt like five minutes, but was probably five seconds, he responded.

"You want to employ me?" He asked.
"Yes."
Q laughed with amusement.
"You wanna give me a job white-boy?"
"Marx." I corrected.

And there it was. On the tip of my tongue, a new name, a new identity. These men didn't know Andy the melancholy valet or Martin the playboy businessman. In this world I was going to be a philosopher like Karl Marx and an activist like Robin Hood...or some bastardized, slightly less moral version. Marx Hood, not a person but a feeling, a whisper, a myth, something that can't be stopped by a bullet, a tank or battleship...an idea.

"You want to give me a job, Marx? All right, let's hear it."

"Like I said, I know that you sell crack and I would like to pay you to...not."

The room went silent, all eyes were on Q.

Q laughed.

He waited a beat for the punchline to the joke I had just told.

 I didn't flinch.

He was quiet for a moment before looking at JD.

"He for real?"

JD nodded.

Q thought for a moment and then with a look and a movement of his hands, he dismissed his crew. They left the room without a word. (He really did run a tight ship). Once we were alone again he spoke.

"And how much are you offering to pay me for this job of ...not selling crack?"

"What you make now, plus twenty five percent. I assume you don't allow anyone else to sell on your corners. That continues, so no one is selling in this neighborhood."

"Customers don't get it from me, they'll just go somewhere else." Q countered.

"Let them." I said flatly.

"Why would I do this?"

"Because you increase profits, decrease work load and lower your risks."

"For how long?"

"As long as I am alive." (Why not give him more incentive?)

I pulled a debit card from my pocket. I set it on the table in front of him.

"This account has $10,000 in it. That is yours for simply listening to us. There's triple that as a bonus, if you take the job, delivered once you open up the books."

"The books?" He asked.

"Yeah, the books. We have to know how much your salary is going to be."

"I took a piece of paper from my pocket and set it next to the card. Here is my phone number and the PIN to the account." I said.

Q was not crazy, I could see this. He knew a good deal when he heard it and if anything I was saying were true, he had to listen. I could see he was considering it, but he needed more time. Another wise choice.

"I appreciate you coming down here to talk to me...Marx was it?"

I nodded.

"I'm going to need some time to consider your proposal."

"Of course."

Q called his soldiers back in and they escorted us out of the building without a word.

JD and I walked in silence. I gazed around me at the graffiti on the walls, dumpsters and street signs, I watched garbage blow past a homeless man. Just down the street a group of young men stared at us for far too long for it to be friendly. I thought to myself that somewhere someone was responsible for this decay. Who was the police chief? Did they even care about this mess? Were police chiefs cycled through every few years, when crime rates inevitably stayed constant, that is to say very high? Why weren't they accountable? Politicians stand up on pedestals a mile high; these people must look like ants from up there. In order to look tough on crime, they make harsher penalties, minimum sentences for this crime or that crime, but it never goes down. Our prisons just fill up. Why do we act like it's doing any good? If Q goes down, someone else will replace him before the cell door closes. Drugs and crime are markets and as long as a market exists desperate people will exploit them, regardless of the risks. So if fear didn't work on these people, what would?

Those of us born with something, anything, can't really relate. It's easy to condemn public welfare and condone parental welfare, when we are the ones getting the handout. How effortless it is for us to think ourselves better than "those" people. What if we were born in this neighborhood? Here, where you are only rewarded for being tough, your education is shit, you see what others just get handed, yet you know that's never coming to you. What do you do? Society tells you to play the game, go to school, get a job, "Work hard and you will succeed". Yet the same people, same families, continue to succeed.

Why? The elitist like to coin terms like "Social Darwinism", this idea that the smartest and most capable people rise to the top. Well that's only true if we all start this race the same, but we don't. We're all playing monopoly only some of us begin the game with Park Place, Boardwalk and two hotels, others start the game here, in a New York City hovel. I can see why those in charge don't want to change the rules, this game isn't fair. If it were really a game you'd quit, but this isn't a game, this is their life and as bad as it gets they still don't quit, they simply adapt and improvise. The smart and the ambitious become Q. In another life this man would have been a doctor, a banker, a leader of industry....In this one he was a crack dealer and an enemy of the state. What if we could change the state? What would he become? What if we changed the rules and turned this into a winnable game, what would happen then?

That's it! That is what I was going to do:

    I was going to change the world!

...well, shoot for the moon, hit the ceiling.

Chapter Seventeen

Captains Of Industry

When my phone rang two days later with a number I didn't recognize, I immediately assumed it was Q. I was right. I was expecting this to happen, in my mind it was the only logical thing for him to do. The checking account that I had opened had been drained, meaning that Q had gotten his pay day and was interested in getting another. I answered the phone and we set up a meeting, as casually as any two businessmen might. I met him over coffee at a Starbucks in Soho. I arrived early and found a seat outside, I looked around, waiting for my guest to arrive and noticed that I could see two other Starbucks' from my vantage point! Man people love coffee...a legal drug, I smirked to myself. My wandering thoughts were interrupted. I saw Q approaching. He sat down, looked at my still bruised face, gave what seemed to be a sincere smile. Then he spoke.

"Sorry about the grill man, my boys worked you over pretty good."

I instinctively touched my lip that was still bruised. An apology, didn't expect that.

"Oh, forget it, it's in the past." I said.

Q nodded.

He waited for me to speak again. I could see in his eyes that he was calculating, taking his time with his responses. A sign of intelligence.

I spoke first.

"I see that you got the money."

"You a cop?" He asked point blank. No doubt just trying to gauge my reaction.

I was a great liar, but telling the truth is even easier.

"No. Do I seem like a cop?" I asked.

"No, you don't. But I don't play and you don't add up. What I can't figure out is how you're trying to set me up."

"That's because I'm not setting you up." I reassured.

"Why would you pay me to not break the law?"

" I never said that. I want to pay you to not sell drugs and to keep others from selling too. Also and more importantly, instead of robbing people, I will pay you to protect them."

Q was silent again. This didn't make sense. I had to reassure him.

"Look, you take money from me. You haven't broken any laws, you stop selling drugs, still nothing against the law. You're going to get the cops off of your back. If you go back to selling, I stop the pay checks. You will be my employee, and everyone still works for you, they just get paid by me. They never have to know."

"Why?" Q asked.

"Because I have the money and you have the manpower and with that we can make your town a decent place to live again."

"Who are you?"

" I am the man you see before you. The one who owns the money tree. If you need a name, how about Marx Hood."

(Yeah, I know the name is a bit obvious, but I was on the spot when I came up with it).

Two hours and three lates later, I got Q to speak quite candidly. His real name was

Lawrence and he had grown up only a few miles from this very spot, had only left New York one time and that was to go to Jersey. After high school he went to college and had even graduated with honors, he studied business management. It became clear to me why he was the leader, he was very smart and very unwilling to take shit from anyone. The more he spoke the more I started to like him, his anger seemed misdirected to me, but I couldn't argue with his logic. People wanted crack, he sold crack. He didn't create the demand, that was white folk who made black folk so poor that the only way they knew how to cope was to smoke crack all day and all he did was fill a role that the world was asking for and he was going to do it just long enough to buy his way out of the ghetto and into something better. It was a war out there and he was a captain. If a few people had to get hurt to accomplish the mission, it was collateral damage. The more he spoke the more I saw him as a true capitalist using the tools at his disposal. Adam Smith would have been proud of his savvy, George Washington would have admired his leadership and bravery in a time of conflict, Thomas Jefferson would have had an illicit and secret affair with his great, great, great, great grandmother. As a matter of fact, he actually had. Yes, this man was as American as apple pie and not killing me the night we met would turn out to be the best decision of his life. I was opportunity knocking and he answered the door.

  The scam…err "business model" was simple at first. I began by purchasing the apartment complex that JD's family lived in, but not outright, I had something vandalized or stolen from the property every day for a month. I met with the owner, a contrary old man named Sal. Sal owned 15 apartment complexes in the neighborhood and this one was now becoming more of a problem than it was worth. He didn't know that I knew he wanted to sell. He also didn't know that I was the one working the recent string of bad luck he was having. I bought a nice new suit (I couldn't get the blood stains out of my last one) and set up the second business meeting of my life. The first was with a drug dealer, this one was with a slum lord.

    We met at the Waldorf for lunch. Our server even recognized me and asked me where I'd been. It was a nice touch to legitimize myself to this man, though I know it didn't matter. The only thing that mattered to Sal was unloading his latest headache without taking a complete bath.

    "Thank you for meeting with me." I began.

"Why do you want my building?" Sal barked.

I smiled, He was a cranky son of a bitch. Kind of reminded me of my grandfather.

" I am looking to buy and develop some real estate as a part of a community restoration movement, some philanthropy that my company takes part..."

He interrupted.

"Philanthropy, sure, great...how much is your company willing to pay for this restoration project?"

"We are willing to offer you...

"...Write it down." He interrupted.

"What?"

"Write down your offer, people can say whatever they want. Doesn't mean shit. My hearing's not as good as it used to be. You write it down there's no misunderstanding."

"OK."

I took out a pen and wrote it down on my napkin, I slid my offer across the table like I had seen done in the movies.

Sal picked up the napkin. His mood immediately turned.

"You're an arrogant son of a bitch!"

I knew that the offer was a bit low, in fact it may have only been about half of what the building was worth. But I knew that he wanted to sell. I also knew that if he didn't sell his "bad luck" was going to continue. I held all of the cards.

We settled on a price about a million dollars below market value, a million dollars! I could turn around and sell it for that much profit. I had essentially made what it takes a working man 30 years to earn, not bad for a mornings work and I made it legitimately...well sort of legitimately. I left the building and made my way on to the hustle and bustle of the city street. I walked through the crowd with a body high that I did not expect, I felt free and strong. My footsteps seemed light as a feather. I was both experiencing and observing at the same time. An odd sphere opened up in the crowd, real or imagined it was separating me from the others sharing the sidewalk. I was a man walking with purpose and, though at that moment I had nowhere to go, I was definitely on my way. Perhaps it was just the high of accomplishment. Maybe it was something just a little bit more...I felt powerful, one thing was certain, it was a feeling I could get used to.

    The next week was spent ironing out the details, I met with Sal's attorneys. They seemed more than a bit surprised that I didn't have a lawyer...or an accountant or anyone else with me to seal a multi-million dollar purchase. I think mostly they just thought it would make getting me to sign all the easier and they were right. Lawyers really slow stuff down. They spoke for what seemed like hours and said a bunch of stuff I didn't really understand. The point I took home was that the sale was final and that I understood the "state" of the building. I smiled politely and signed the papers they put in front of me well aware that I was buying a dilapidated slum. By the end of the day I was the proud owner of my first apartment building! I have to admit I was a little proud. I went back to the building and looked it up and down. Rain stained brick, several windows were broken and simply taped back together by the residents. The stairs leading up to it were worn to the point of being a hazard. It didn't look like much, but it would and it was mine.

    A few days later I was on my way out the door when I overheard Mary talking to one of her neighbors.

"So get this, you know the guy that owns the building, Sal?"

"Yeah."

"He sold it."

"No?"

"New owner's changing the rent." Mary said.

"What? We got rent control, he can't do that!"

"I know honey, get this, he's lowering it...by half!"

It was true, I found out that I could pay the upkeep and taxes on the place and still turn a small profit charging half the rent...Half! I didn't feel so bad about taking it to ole Sal now...greedy, greedy.

I couldn't help but smile. Most of these people were good hardworking folks, a few were rude and maybe a bit racist, but all in all they were nice and I definitely noticed a difference in everyone after the sale. They were friendlier and more lighthearted. The reduction in rent seemed to correlate directly to a reduction in stress. Who couldn't use some extra cash every month for their bills or something they enjoy?

    I didn't stop with the rent, about a third of the tenants didn't have jobs and a lot of others needed more work. So I made JD the new building manager and hired the tenants to help restore the building. I repainted the whole thing, replaced all the windows, repaved the steps, and did a ton of plumbing work. It turns out that a plumber lived right in the building, it was perfect. The place was really shaping up. I was taking pride in watching it get nicer every week.

    With the extra money Mary was saving on rent, plus the substantial salary we had set JD up with, little Janie was able to see a specialist about her lungs. With the treatment she was feeling better all the time, her cough had gone away and her energy was way up. Every time I stepped through that door she was sure to sprint up to me and give my leg a big hug. She was so healthy and full of life now, it melted my heart every time I saw her.

My next question was, what was I to do with all of Q's "employees"? Some of them I'd met and they were good at heart, others were just violent, sociopaths who weren't in the game for the money. They were in it because they were slow witted and uneducated and being dealers, they got to act like big shots and push people around like bouncers or...cops! That's it! This would be my police force! It seemed so obvious now.

With a few phone calls and some dollar bills changing hands, it was on. It didn't take long for them to go to work either. One night a couple of teens were vandalizing the side of our building near where we kept the dumpster. They were caught in the act by a guy named "Sugs". He was a mean dude and one of Q's people, so he was on the payroll. I'm not sure exactly what tactics he took, but he scared the living daylights out of them. The three boys showed up the very next day to clean up the spray paint and apologize to JD. Word must have traveled too, because it never happened again.

It was all working wonderfully. We had a few setbacks and there was still a little random crime. All in all though all of the ex-drug dealers we were employing were making for one bad-ass neighborhood-watch program. Q was efficient and powerful. Very little happened in his neighborhood that he wasn't aware of.

The property value in this neighborhood and any neighborhood really, was largely dependent on the crime. I now controlled the majority of the crime. Nothing serious, mostly break-ins, vandalism, petty theft, I was clear that I didn't want anyone hurt. There were a few rogue criminals willing to hurt people who wandered into "our" town, which at this time was about five square blocks. These rogues didn't last long though. Q and his merry men would make certain of that. I increased the crime in an area I was interested in buying. When the owners could no longer stand to put up with the maintenance of their property, Marx Hood under the investment group Van Sant and Associates, would swoop in and relieve them of the burden of property ownership. At a substantially reduced price of course. Soon after the acquisition the crime would go back to normal and business would continue as usual.

It was amazingly simple and effective. The properties of Van Sant and Associates were growing by the month. We were quickly becoming the kings of Harlem. And not so slowly Harlem was turning into a much nicer place to live.

    After a time I felt as though I had overstayed my welcome with JD and his family. I was getting to be known around the building (I was the only white guy) and neighborhood, mostly as JD's friend. JD and Q were the only ones privy to my true standing in the community. I was OK with not getting the credit and I liked where I lived, but I was also a bit weary. I saw a documentary once about this guy called the Grizzly Man. The movie was about this eccentric fellow who moved into the middle of the Alaskan wilderness and started living with the grizzlies in an attempt to save them from people. The footage was astounding and this group of bears actually did accept him into their world. Everything was going smoothly until one day a bear from outside the region wandered into the group and was not familiar with this guy and only saw him as food. The bear ate him. To me it was an allegory. I was growing more popular all the time, but I wasn't ready to act like I owned this place. Not everyone here was going to accept me as one of their own, no matter what. So JD became the face of my business, and Q the head of my "security". I stayed behind the scenes and worked my magic from the outside.

  I rented a nice place overlooking Central Park. It was right near where Yoko Ono lived. It was large and spacious with big bright windows. I liked to sit and look out over the city at the little people down there, keeping themselves busy.

I began to play the part of a New York City businessman quite well. This amazing penthouse was a start, but I still got my hair cut by a guy named Sammy. He was in his sixties and had been cutting hair his whole life; he worked out of a place near JD's apartment in a building I owned actually. He was always in good spirits, but when we lowered his rent something changed in him for certain, he just moved a little easier, as if he'd been quietly carrying a great burden his whole life and now it was gone. I'll never forget the very next time I went to see him he showed off some new shears that he'd bought "With these, now the job can get done right!" he told me with pride. It felt good to see him so happy and to know I had a small part in it. The cheap hair cut was about the only cheap thing I kept though and the truth was I mostly kept it so I had an excuse to come see Sammy and check up on things in "our" town.

    I started wearing designer suits, suits that were just silly expensive, but I had to keep up appearances. Well, this is what I told myself, but the truth is I kind of liked it. I felt strong and confident wearing clothes that cost more than most men make in a month. People treated you differently too. For no good reason I felt like people were kinder and more respectful...ah the power of perception. I was just a middle class kid from Utah, well I used to be anyway. It was hard for me to pin-point when it happened, but I was definitely changing. I felt different now, though maybe I always was. Who just picks up a bag of money lying next to the blood-soaked corpse of a drug dealer and leaves the country with it? Wouldn't most people just call the police? Oddly enough all of these years had passed since that night and I'd never really given it much thought. I suppose I just assumed that everyone in my situation would do the same, but would they? I had come so far and now I was dressed just like the people I used to hate when I was parking cars. I wasn't them though, I was a man with a plan, I lowered rent, restored buildings and you can be damn sure I was a good tipper! I was a good person. I could believe this just as long as I didn't think too hard about the past.

Chapter Eighteen

A Political Animal

I looked up at the clock on the wall, then back to my phone, yup the time was correct. A huge table stretched out in front of me and several well-dressed gentlemen were working out the details of my latest acquisition. One of the men was my new lawyer, an old curmudgeon named Art Charles of Charles and Associates, he was in his mid sixties but hadn't lost any fire, well if he had I would have liked to see what he was in his youth, because today that son of a bitch was a real hard ass and a shrewd negotiator. He billed me five hundred dollars an hour and easily saved me a thousand. Yeah, he was worth every penny. I'm glad he was on my team, as often as not I would just send him as proxy to finish the deals. I was a business-man of sorts, but really most business bored the hell out of me. Instead I preferred to find a nice bench in Central Park to sit and read or wander around and people watch. New York was a great place for that.

    I still kept a watchful eye on the reclamation of my buildings and met with JD once in a while to discuss our plans or just life. He'd met a pretty girl named Stacy, she was a grad-student in social work at NYU, just his style. So I saw less and less of him these days and when we did meet it was to discuss business. I spent more and more time with Q. It was odd to me how we had grown up in such different worlds but had a lot in common.

Conversations were easy with him. He looked like a bad man, and in many ways he was...but it was hard for me to see him as anything less than a leader willing to make hard choices that may even get people hurt or killed. How was he different than a general? I wondered. He didn't get any medals and his budget was smaller, but he was protecting our streets, in much more obvious ways than the constant wars our generals were fighting in oil rich lands half-way around the world.

    Q really did like to play pool. He and I would go out to the bar and shoot stick all night sometimes. At first it was just to talk shop, lately it was just because we liked it. I wasn't like anyone he knew and he enjoyed bouncing ideas off of me. He was a different person when he didn't have to keep up appearances around his soldiers. He would come down to my place and watch old Star Trek episodes. It was an odd relationship and admittedly I liked going places with him, especially back in the old neighborhood. He was very respected, feared, and when I went around with him, by proxy I was respected and feared. It was a foreign experience to me, but I liked it. When we walked the streets people moved out of *our* way.

My place wasn't far from the Metropolitan Museum of Art. The entry fee was based on donation. All of these astounding works of art and pieces of history right here in one place for the world to see. There is no way that you could turn a profit charging a few dollars a head, the works were priceless. If they wanted to make a profit they'd have to charge 500 bucks a head. I suppose that's what governments are for, to provide things that are good for all but not good for profit.

I spent a fair amount of time down there. I would wander around the museum and conjure up ideas on how to expand our holdings and influence. Again, it seemed so easy when you didn't have to play by the rules. The rules made things hard and the laws started to seem as though they were just set up to make those who followed them fail.

I never felt bad about running the property values down on the buildings. No one really owned them, well at least no one near this neighborhood. Karl Marx once wrote "The capitalist will defend private property ownership to the death! Yet ninety-nine percent of them own nothing." He may have been on to something. Even most people who "own" a house, actually only own a mortgage. My father once told me that if you want to find out who really owns the property, stop paying the taxes on it.

So if the people who lived in the homes and ran the businesses didn't own them, who did? No one in Harlem. You have to have quite a bit of money to own a building on Manhattan Island, even if it is in a rough part of Harlem. If you had money, no way you're living up here. No, the people who owned Harlem lived in Soho, the Hamptons, Malibu, South Beach, Saudi Arabia, China or more likely had homes many places, but not here.

    It's always easier to take advantage of those faceless entities that are the "owners". I left alone the mom and pop shops and as often as not I would buy the building they were leasing. At this point they were subject to the Marx Hood discount on rent. It was roughly half, sometimes more, sometimes less. But always less than they had been paying. This in turn gave those shop-keepers more money that they would spend, where might you ask? That's right, in Harlem.

It was fantastic to watch how quickly things were changing and time seemed to fly by. I had actually been living in New York for a full two years before I knew it. I was becoming a real estate magnate. As time passed though I could tell that there was only so much I could do, even with the millions I was making. Much of that money was now tied up into assets. We still needed help keeping the roads paved and the sidewalks clean. In short we needed to start pumping from the public well. I suggested that JD should run for office. The state senator in our district was a guy named Maurice Brockman and he had been hanging on to the seat by a thread and while he tried to claim most of the credit for the improvements that were happening all around him, we had a secret weapon, a local football legend.

Chapter Nineteen

The Campaign Trail

It wasn't hard to convince JD to jump on board. He was young, charismatic and honestly wanted to make a difference, all the attributes of someone new to politics. He also wanted to distance himself from the stuff that Q and I were into, which really wasn't a bad idea. We were making the neighborhood nicer, but we were breaking the law to do it. JD's girl Stacy was a big help too, she told us that she thought it was his "calling". I'm not sure I believe in callings, but he did have the tools to win. His father had been a local celebrity and JD had lead his high school to their first and only state championship. JD's Aunt had lived there her whole life and had an incredible number of connections. It seemed odd to me that for a woman who knew so many people who liked her and were willing to help, she had never gotten further in life. I suppose that having connections to a whole bunch of people who aren't connected has little value. They were all in luck now, they had an edge that they'd never had before, a connection to some real money.

    The process seemed a bit overwhelming at first, so we hired a campaign manager, Marie Swanson. I don't know if she was good or not, but she sure spoke like she knew what she was doing and was very confidant that we could win. I shared her confidence, but I'm not sure why. The momentum for what JD, Q and I were building was speeding up and people around us started to believe; confidence is infectious.

We jumped into the race late, but played catch up rather well. At the first debate, Senator Brockman looked like a tired old politician regurgitating the same rhetoric and JD came across as witty and charming, a breath of fresh air. It could not have gone better. The truth was JD and the senator were saying pretty much the exact same thing, its just that JD was...I don't know, funnier, I guess. Politics is weird, it seems that not much changes from high school elections (JD was his class president as well). It's still more about popularity than any real issues.

We gained in the polls quickly and surpassed the incumbent. In one of the stranger conversations that I had ever had, Q told me that he could "guarantee" that JD would win if I wanted. I don't know what his plans were exactly, though I knew that threats of violence, extortion and even murder were things that Q was capable of. I assured him that we could win this one legitimately and that any other "tactics" would just draw unwanted attention. He agreed to do things my way, but I never forgot what he was offering.

When election night came, JD won by a landslide. He was smart and funny and attractive, it was all he needed (We also outspent the former Senator Brockman seven to one...ahh democracy at work!)

We had our foot in the door. We now had a voice and could try to steer the ship of government to a course slightly closer to the one we desired. It was still going to be hard to get things done as fast as we would have liked, but this was a fantastic start...though in many ways it meant the end of my friendship with JD. Our time together became more about business.

Between his new career, and Stacy, to whom he'd recently become engaged, there wasn't much time for us. Besides, I wasn't the same guy he used to know. I had changed so much and while he needed me, he also needed distance from me. I was willing to do whatever it took to accomplish my goals, but now as a part of the machine he needed to work more and more within the confines of the rule of law. It suited him, he was a moral person and believed in the system. This was a fundamental difference between us.

So he was now State Senator John Daniels. Wow, it had quite a ring to it. It was hard to believe that not long ago he was an accomplice in a burglary that netted us millions. Come to think of it, none of this would have been possible had he not. I didn't think about it much but I was a little surprised that nothing ever came of that robbery. It was a lot of money, although there is a good chance that it wasn't reported to the police because it wasn't supposed to exist. One of the risks you take when you dodge taxes I suppose. But my surprise wasn't just about the money. For a while now Q and I had been staging crimes in neighborhoods we were interested in investing in. There was some serious racketeering going on and I hadn't heard a peep about it from any authority. I guess I expected that after a while it would look suspicious that the acquisitions of Van Sant and Associates always revolved around buying properties that were experiencing abrupt increases in crime rates and vandalism. But nothing, at least not yet. I always suspected something like that would be hard to prove. I was beginning to realize that cops pretty much only collect the low hanging fruit. Smart people rarely get caught, in fact, smart people just change the rules so that what they are doing is no longer against the law. This is what I learned as the crew and I got more and more involved in the world of politics, JD was a quick study and we were off and running.

Chapter Twenty
House Bill # 342

I quickly became used to getting my own way. I had the money and the political connections to get things done. I had a hand in getting roads re-paved, streetlights replaced, allocation of funds for schools, you name it and if it was happening in Harlem, Marx Hood had a hand in it. Of course no one knew this. I was simply a lobbyist for a state senator and a local New York City businessman as far as anyone was concerned. JD had become incredibly adept at convincing his cohorts in government to see things our way and the ones that didn't, well Q and I would take care of those; nothing violent, though when Q was involved the threat of it always existed. No, mostly it was just a campaign contribution here, a promise to vote for their bill there and a little blackmail once in a while.

Our latest venture was House Bill #342. It was the talk of the nation, people either loved it or hated. It was absolutely the most comprehensive piece of Healthcare legislation that this country had ever seen. The supporters deemed it the "Right to Health Act". Not to be out-done, its detractors called it the "The Right to Death Act". The death these people were talking about was the death of the economy that would of course result if it became law.

The bill was wildly popular with sick people and just as unpopular with insurance companies. With the sympathy that JD and I had experienced in seeing little Janie sick all the time and knowing this bill could help tens of thousands of kids just like her, it quickly became our focus.

This controversial piece of legislation had narrowly passed the House and was now being debated in a very divided Senate. For weeks it seemed imminent that it was going to fail...that is until we intervened with our own tactics. There were three Senators on the fence who had been elected by huge donations from insurance companies. JD and I had been through every single word of that exhaustive bill and we were convinced it was the right thing to do. So one by one we addressed the dissenters.

Senator Thorn from Idaho had based his campaign on his high moral character, as a former minister. It didn't take us long to find his mistresses... and his illegitimate children.

Some photos and an anonymous phone call with the threat of exposure and voila!…the Senator changed his tune and started caring about sick children. Of course when he made the announcement that he'd changed his mind, it was because he'd prayed about it. What a guy.

Next on our list was Senator Brooks from Missouri. This guy was easy to convince, but not cheap. All we had to do was make a bigger donation to his campaign than the insurance companies had and let me tell you, it was sizable. I never met with him directly as the money really wasn't a donation but in fact a bribe. We made sure there was plenty of evidence of the transaction so that later we could blackmail him to get it back. One more to go and things were looking good. I was the brains, JD was the face and Q was the muscle behind a Leviathan that couldn't be stopped.

Only one thing stood in our way, James Clifton.

From all accounts Senator Clifton was a self-made man. He started off swinging a hammer before he opened his first construction company at twenty-three. By thirty it was the largest in Ohio. Clifton construction now had assets exceeding two billion dollars. As far as we could tell, he was a straight shooter, no dirt was to be found. He was a man of principle and while he couldn't see the trees through the forest, he stood up for what he believed in. I had to respect him for that. The only real problem with him was that he had been rich too long and had lost the ability to understand the value of a dollar and how crippling healthcare costs can be to an average family. In short, we had no play.

This man was one of the most powerful men in the United States, the senate majority leader, a man who some day may be president. After Van Sant and Associates made a sizable donation to his re-election campaign, I was able to get some face time with the distinguished gentleman. I spent a week before the meeting practicing my pitch in the mirror. When the day arrived I was ready and laid it all out there, I gave him my very best. It was elegant and succinct, the words flowed through me with the passion I truly possessed on why this piece of healthcare legislation was monumental and would save the lives of thousands of Americans. I *needed* him to change his mind. He was polite and listened without interruption and when I was finished he offered a rebuttal, a very condescending rebuttal. He wasn't intimidated by me. He should have been. He spoke with the tone of a lion humoring a gazelle, but he was the gazelle. To him I was just some lobbyist, the kind he answered questions for everyday. The questions he answered today on the surface were about healthcare, but they were actually determining how long he would live. The man across from me was the one barrier between this country and sweeping healthcare reform that would benefit everyone but the very, very rich. This legislation, would ultimately save the lives of thousands and thousands of men, women and children. One life to save thousands, was it really a choice? In war, if faced with the same decision, it would be tantamount to treason to even consider letting this man go. He carried no gun, wore no military fatigues, but this man could kill people through his action, or inaction as easy as any warlord. He was not a bad person, he had made his money honestly as far as my best research had indicated. Like all good Senators, he cheated on his wife, the only difference was everyone knew it (including his wife) and didn't care. This left me with no leverage over him. He was an anomaly, a man with good intentions, but a loss of perspective. His philosophy was different than mine, he wanted change, just not this change. He was a man of his convictions and would not be swayed by anyone. He never had to compromise. He held all of the cards, all of them but one.

One month from that day Senator James Clifton died from a massive heart attack. It wasn't shocking to the nation, he had a history of heart problems, but by no means had he died from natural causes. He died from something I had put into his morning tea.

Like all modern heroes I had killed an innocent man. There was no duel, no struggle or fight, I wasn't even in the same state when it happened, but he was dead and I had killed him.

I was surprised by how I felt when I heard the news that he was dead. When I had made the decision to put the hit out on a Senator, I didn't do it lightly, but I considered it practical. James Clifton was an obstinate old man, but a good man and his life had value. Without the late Senator, the bill passed the Senate, was signed by the President and became law. The underhanded and violent actions we had taken, had in no small way, created a better, longer life for millions of people.

What a world.

Chapter Twenty-One

The Rising Star

I looked out among the crowd of thousands that had gathered below. They were all here for us. JD's campaign manager Marie stood at the podium a few feet away giving a speech. The crowd cheered with delight at every word she said. I wonder if they were even listening? I stood on the stage next to JD. He held his new wife Stacy's hand, both of them looked incredible. JD glanced over at me, he smirked and slightly shook his head. He couldn't believe where he was right now, it was hard for me to believe too.

The speech continued.

"They said we couldn't do it..."

I found myself drifting from the present moment. My mind never at peace for long, began to dart to pieces of information dormant in my brain. It began to connect dots in ways it never had before, quite literally as new dendrites were forming connections to neurons in my brain. A simple and profound question appeared in my mind:

"What am I doing?"

What drives a man to acquire more than he needs? The sparkle of gold has long lost the luster to the eyes of the wealthy. A mansion is merely a place to sleep. A five star meal, only tasty food soon forgotten. Why then do we not stop as millionaires... most of us can only dream of what that kind of wealth would bring and yet some have thousands of millions of dollars. Why keep going?

A child squeals with delight from knocking over a stack of blocks. She did something. The world was one way, it had a stack of blocks in it, and now it was another. Are we all in a race to see who can knock over (or build) the biggest stack of blocks? By asserting will we change things; by changing things we prove to others that we matter. But what is the end game? Why do we need to matter to others? To people we don't know, people we will never know. Is it as simple as sex appeal? Do we want wealth, power and six pack abs for the same reason? A reproductive advantage? What is a leader? Are these men and women who truly believe they know what's best for us? Do they care *so* much that they are willing to dedicate their lives to making ours better? Or are they trying to matter? Trying to feed the insatiable monster that is the human ego. Beneath it all, are they only trying to fill an emptiness? An emptiness that is caused by the need to matter, the need for approval, the addiction-like craving for meaning in a life that may have no meaning, save the ones that we choose to attach to it. Most leaders in history have come from places of great material wealth, their desires are not so easy to define.

    The problem may be that we seek to fill the void with objects that have no volume. They take no space and there is no answer to the question: Is this enough?

    When do we have enough friends, enough approval, enough force of will...when do we matter? Perhaps by looking outward in search of these answers we are looking in the wrong place. Maybe we only need to matter to one person?

I watched as Marie delivered that speech, the crowd hung on her every word. Because of me, all of this was because of me. We were so high, the people looked like ants from up here…I seem to remember that thought from before. An echo from a former life.

There I stood, a lover, a liar, a humanist, a murderer, a businessman and racketeer, I was a philanthropist, a lobbyist, a gangster, a politician, a player. I was loved and hated, rich beyond the imagination of those below.

"May I introduce to you the next Senator from New York!!!" Marie shouted with fervor.

The massive crowd roared with zeal!

I was a philosopher king...a benevolent villain...and I was exactly what this world needed.

The End.

Made in the USA
San Bernardino, CA
25 June 2018